The La
Lady Continues

Devotions Inspired by Nature

MW01609016

Swamp People, A&E Television Networks LLC, 2022

Job A Story of Unlikely Joy, 2018 Lisa Harper Published by Lifeway Press

Hacksaw Ridge 2016 Cosmos Filmed Entertainment Pty Ltd.

The Final Testament of the Holy Bible, 2011 James Frey Published by Gagosian Gallery

Eagle When She Flies, written by Dolly Parton, 1991 Sony Music Entertainment Inc.

Be A Light, written by Thomas Rhett, Matt Dragstrem, Josh Miller, Josh Thompson, 2020 Big Machine Label Group

Table of Contents

Welcome

Welcome

If this is your first time reading one of these, it all started with a nudge from God, a forgotten iPod, and a lawnmower. Being a visual learner, God has taken my lawnmowing and snow blowing exploits and used them as a teaching opportunity to draw me closer to Him. After I told a friend about them, they recommended that I write them down and share them and so I did.

It's hard to believe that I have been writing these devotionals for over four years now. It feels like the first one was just yesterday. This journey with God, the lawnmower, snowblower, and myself has had its ups and downs, but I would not have missed a single moment of it. I absolutely love how God has moved in my life and continued to guide me through the cycles of growth in our relationship.

My hope and prayer is that through these, your relationship with our Savior will grow and that He might ignite a passion to study and learn His written words for us. My drive to study the Bible and learn the truths that God has for me is a big part of why I write, and I pray that these can be used by God to fan the flame of whatever gifting lies within you.

Enjoy!

Lisa

Compassion in the Gap

God gave me this title on Wednesday as I was driving in to work, and I wondered what He was trying to tell me. I got to the office, did my morning routine and then clicked on the latest YouTube sermon in my subscribed list and the speaker began to talk about compassion. The next video in the list, compassion. The next video, being a bridge, aka standing in the gap. Later I discovered that a friend had sent me their morning devotional on compassion. I thought it would be over when I raised my hands in submission and said I would dive in, but Thursday was filled with more videos, devotionals, and seminars where compassion and being willing to stand in complicated places was the main focus.

And this morning... God spoke...

"Compassion is about allowing someone to speak words that make your blood boil and choosing to love them instead of escalating with blood boiling words of your own."

How do I educate in the arenas You have called me to without the escalation?

"You follow My lead and speak My words. Using fear or anger as an educational tool has temporary results but will eventually lead My believers astray and I can't allow that. Truth in love takes time to sink in but has lasting and permanent results."

It's hard to not fight back when the daggers fly!

"Yes, it is. But you have to recognize that when people attack, they are not attacking you, they are attacking Me and the convictions they are fighting to deny. I am your front and rear shield, and I will never leave you!"

Standing in the gap has meant that people from both sides have argued their point to the fullest in an attempt to get me to chose one over the other. That's not what God has called me to, He has called me to stand firmly in the middle; to be one of many pillars that will hold up the bridge connecting each side. Seeing the divisiveness and anger being tossed around so flippantly absolutely breaks my heart. If it does this to me, I can't imagine how God feels when He sees the way we behave.

I understand now what He is asking of me and many of you. He's asking us to love not to retaliate. He's asking us to represent the truth with integrity not with venom. He's asking us to be His image bearer, the one who can feel the pain and desperation of each side knowing that God is taking them on a journey just like us.

No matter what gap God has you standing in, trust that He is at work in it and lives are being changed by your willingness to simply stand. Yes, it hurts at times, yes, you want to scream at the top of your lungs at times. Let God's love be the strength that fills your shoulders. Let His grace be your deflector shield. Stand strong my friend and most importantly, have compassion in the gap!

Philippians 2:1-2
Therefore if you have any encouragement from being united with Christ, if any comfort from his love, if any common sharing in the Spirit, if any tenderness and compassion, then make my joy complete by being like-minded, having the same love, being one in spirit and of one mind.

Listen to Him

Going to do things a little differently again. Normally I finish with a Scripture, but today I'm going to start with it. I may still end with it, but it's more important to see if upfront. The passage comes from my favorite chapter of my favorite book of the Bible; anyone who knows me is shouting MARK 9, she's going to Mark 9... and they would be right lol. In the beginning of this chapter, Jesus has taken Peter, James, and John to the mount of transfiguration and in verse 7 God speaks to the three of them, *"Then a cloud appeared and covered them, and a voice came from the cloud: 'This is my Son, whom I love, listen to him!'"* Now before you read any further, take a moment and let three words from that verse sink deeply into your soul, "listen to him."

As I sheepishly raise my hand, are any of you convicted by those words?

He doesn't say, talk to him, or argue with him, or ask him any question under the sun. He didn't say tell him what you want him to do. No, He said LISTEN to him. Two events have happened to me in the last 24 hours that resonate my disobedience to those 3 little yet powerful words...

Last night was the final night of an Empowered Women Study that I helped my super amazing friend Chelsea lead. We made plans to do the last one together and went back and forth with a few e-mails to where I thought we agreed to do it at her church. It's a little bit of a drive for me, so I felt nudged to text her before I left to make sure we were set, but I didn't want to bug her, so I didn't. I got to the church about 15 minutes early and felt nudged to text her how cute her church was, but again, I didn't listen. So ONE minute before the LIVE event is supposed to start, she's not there, so I text her to find out where she was. Only to discover that she assumed since I didn't email her back that we weren't going to do it together, and she was all set to do it at home by herself. It all worked out fine, we joked about it, and just started the study late, but I should have listened.

So now you're thinking, "she's learned her lesson, she won't make that mistake again." WRONG! Less than 24 hours later I head out to mow the lawn. Now I mow the lower field by the lake and with all of the rain it's really wet down there so I have to be careful. I actually can't mow the entire lower field because of the wetness, I can only do part of it. I heard the voice whisper, "don't go any further, only mow to this point." Once again, I ignored the voice and went a solid 20 yards further. It worked for a few passes, and then... the mower slows... tires spin... I'm STUCK! As I'm trying to undo what I've done, I can hear Jesus laughing hard saying, "baby I told you to turn, why didn't you listen? I'm trying to help you, not hurt you, listen to me when I speak."

Why are those 3 words SO HARD?

I want to be faithful, but my stubborn pride gets me in more

trouble than I care to admit. I KNOW His voice, I knew it was HIM, but I chose to ignore it. How about you? When are we going to be willing to lay it ALL down and listen? He is a faithful, loving, caring, trustworthy God. His desire for us is to strive to live a life worthy of what He has called us to. He LOVES us so much that He paid a price meant for us to pay.

When He speaks LISTEN TO HIM! He won't let you down.

Mark 9:7
Then a cloud appeared and covered them, and a voice came from the cloud: "This is my Son, whom I love, listen to him!"

I Will Make You Love Me

A few days ago, we brought a new puppy into our family, and our older dog is not so sure about our decision to do this. Jake, the puppy, is determined to make Tyler, our 8-year-old, love him. He tries to play, lick, and snuggle but has gotten snubbed... until today. While Tyler is still not completely sure, he is now willing to play tug-o-war, let Jake chase his tail, and share treats, but still not ready to snuggle. Jake is refusing to give up hope.

Watching these two got me thinking...

This is exactly like our relationship with God. He tries to get us to have a complete relationship with Him and we take forever, giving just a little of ourselves at a time. What's wild is that God is more determined with us than Jake will be with Tyler. Soon Jake will be satisfied with what he can get out of the relationship, but God will never be satisfied until we surrender completely.

That knowledge brings peace to my heart. I, like so many, struggle trusting, especially God. The pain of my past will sometimes create a doubt that God could love someone like me. But God never stops reaching out. He never stops placing His hand on my shoulder and whispering in my ear how much He loves me.

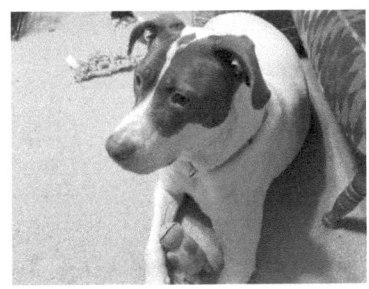

That's what He does for each and every one of us. His desire is for ALL of us to be saved!

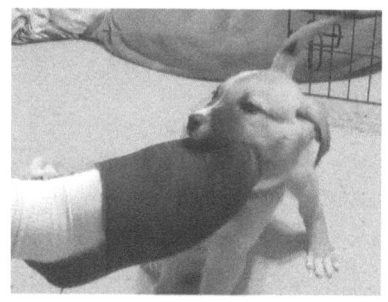

No matter what your struggle is… No matter what you've gone through… GOD IS THERE! Jesus is that friend who sticks closer than a brother. His faithfulness will outlast your resistance.

Listen to His call… Celebrate His love… Rest in His arms…

HIS LOVE WILL NEVER FAIL YOU!

1 Corinthians 1:8-9
He will also keep you firm to the end, so that you will be blameless on the day of our Lord Jesus Christ. God is faithful, who has called you into fellowship with his Son, Jesus Christ our Lord.

Love Talks Loudly

Lately, living on the lake, we have seen some of the most incredible sunsets. On Christmas night we were all blessed with an amazing sunset. I happened to be walking up to the house to feed the dogs, so I was privileged to see it from start to finish. As I was looking over those photos as well as some from another sunset, God hit me with three simple yet profound words, "Love talks loudly."

Usually I hear the words "You're welcome," but not this time. It took me a few minutes to work it out, but, as usual, God was right, love talks loudly, especially when it comes directly from Him. Nature is how He grabs my attention the most; it's both a disciplinary tool and a gift giving tool that He wields like the master image maker He is. Over the last few years, as my relationship with Him has grown, the photographic memories have gotten way more intense, and my spirit is routinely overwhelmed with the beauty found within.

When we listen and look for it, God's love for us speaks so loudly it can bust an eardrum! I wonder what would happen if we showed the same love for others that God lavishes on us? Christmas may be over, but our attitudes don't have to revert back to the pre-Christmas "me first" mentality; my prayer for all of us is that we remember who we are and WHOSE we are.

Remember when you let someone go in front of us at the store because it's Christmas? Or maybe you spoke a little sweeter to that person you disagree with just to show a little holiday spirit? Let's not forget how loudly love speaks if you let it. I've heard this statement a lot lately, "love accomplishes more than hate ever dreamed possible." And it's so true. We have the ability to change the world one LOVING word at a time. It doesn't matter what someone does or says to you, what matters is how you respond.

My goal for the coming year…
LET LOVE SPEAK LOUDLY IN
AND THROUGH ME.

Join me!

Proverbs 22:11
One who loves a pure heart and who speaks with grace will have the king for a friend.

The Jesus Priority

Summertime is usually a busy time on the lake, and today was no

different. Much needed coffee with a friend, birthday shopping, lawn mowing, garden prep, writing, plant watering, tree and bush trimming... and the list goes on and on. Sometimes I get a little jealous when I see people out on the lake fishing or skiing, but I wouldn't trade the life I have for anything.

In the middle of the first mow of the season God spoke...

"Tell me how you prioritized your list for today."

Coffee with my friend always drives me closer to you, so that one was a no brainer, had to make that happen. I had time before I met with her to get Tyler's eye drops done, let both dogs out, and do a little Bible studying and writing. When I got home, Bob had just finished work, and we had to decide what all to do next. I knew if I tried to mow before we went shopping, I would be thinking about all that needed to be done instead of listening to You teach, so we did all our shopping first. While I mowed, Bob worked

on the garden, and that left us time to trim some trees and bushes before the light faded.

"There seemed to be a lot of focus on me in your prioritizing. Do you do that every day?"

No, sometimes the checklist is overwhelming, and I just jump in and start checking things off as quickly as I can.

"Did I help you accomplish your list today?"

Yes

"Don't you think I would do the same on your super busy days?"

Can't you be wrong just once?

"Haha, I love you too."

What does your priority list look like? Are you letting Jesus direct your steps? I have to admit, as busy as today was, we got a lot done, and I know it had nothing to do with my abilities. It was solely because of our reliance on Jesus that all those things were accomplished.

Trust the One who makes it all happen.

Let Him guide your day.

He IS faithful!

Proverbs 3:5-6
Trust in the Lord with all your heart, and do not rely on your own insight. In all your ways acknowledge him, and he will make straight your paths.

Terminology of Love

A few weeks ago, my husband found a frog while he was chopping and stacking wood. He called me out to see it because he thought it was a toad with a really weird underbelly. He was shocked when I said that it was a tree frog, and the yellow skin on the underside of his back legs was a protective feature to make predators think they are poisonous. Now before you go there, I have been handling reptiles for 50 years and I know the necessity of hand washing and not touching my eyes etc. Now, the reptile nerd in me really wanted to know if this was a Cope's Grey Tree Frog, or an Eastern Grey Tree Frog, so I started researching the differences between the two.

My husband was looking over my shoulder while I was researching a few things and he started laughing and asking if I understood what I was reading. The research paper I was reading was loaded with fancy words like cryptic diploid-tetraploid, versicolor, post-metamorphic migrations, etc. I raised and bred different reptiles, including tree frogs, for years, so, through research I learned the different terminology used.

In the middle of all my research God spoke…

"Why are complex words so important?"

I think people feel it makes them look smart and therefore more valuable.

"Don't they realize they are priceless no matter how many big words they know? I love them and they are my children."

Sometimes we want the world to know so that we can feel it.

"When will I be enough?"

Ouch! I know I get caught up in using fancy words a lot. There's so 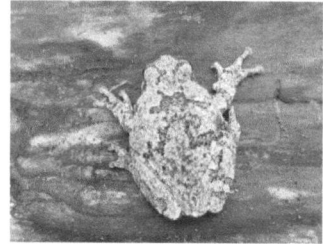 many churchy words that make me feel smart just because I know what they mean, but that's not where my value comes from. My value comes from a God who loved me when I struggled in science class. He loved me when I was so intoxicated, I couldn't put a complete sentence together. He loves me despite ALL of my shortcomings.

And He loves you the same! He thinks you are the BOMB!

Put your faith in Him, not in the small things this world has to offer.

Oh, and just in case you were wondering... it's a Cope's Grey Tree Frog. The only way to tell the difference is in the flutter or trill in their mating call, not their appearance.

Matthew 16:24-26
Then Jesus told his disciples, "If any wish to come after me, let them deny themselves and take up their cross and follow me. For those who want to save their life will lose it, and those who lose their life for my sake will find it. For what will it profit them if they gain the whole world but forfeit their life? Or what will they give in return for their life?

The Bible Everyone Reads

There's this show on the History Channel that Bob and I like to watch called "Swamp People." It's about people who live in the swamps of Louisiana and hunt alligators during the 30-day hunting season. Hunting alligators provides half of their yearly income, which is not much, but that's not what caught my attention with the show. They have what they call "swamp rules" which in a nutshell means, if a neighbor is in need, you drop everything to help them. It doesn't matter how busy you are, it doesn't matter if it's the last day of the season and you still have tags to fill, if a friend needs help you stop and help them. Their neighbors won't go hungry, or do without, because each life and friendship matter more than their own.

Last season due to the influx of alligator farms, the price for the skins was cut by two thirds and it threatened a more than a century long lifestyle. Instead of hanging their heads and quitting, hunters who used to fiercely compete against each other, banded together, pooled their resources and started processing the alligators themselves and selling the meat to local restaurants. Instead of their way of life dying out, they found a way to make it thrive again by setting aside their competitive nature and working together. As a cold front moved in, they knew they had to tag out early because alligators don't feed when temperatures drop. While most could do that with ease, there was one hunter who knew he couldn't do it in 24 hours. So, again, they stopped and helped. They split the tags up between the boats and all of the hunters were able to hunt the required alligators before the cold front moved in and ended their season early.

When I stopped to really look at it, these men and women live out the Bible each and every day of their lives. As their normal way of life, they do what most of us have a tendency to struggle with. They think of others before themselves and go out of their way help ANYONE in need. Many would marginalize this people group, but I stand in awe of them, and I'm desperate to learn from them.

There's a quote that I see from time to time, "You are the only Bible some people will ever read." How we visibly live out our faith can change someone's view of God. Those "swamp people" model a life of love, grace, and community the way ALL Christians are called to. I want to live that way myself. I want people to draw close the Jesus as a result of seeing Him guide my every move.

What about you? What type of Bible do you want people to see in you?

Acts 1:8
But you will receive power when the Holy Spirit comes on you; and you will be my witnesses in Jerusalem, and in all Judea and Samaria, and to the ends of the earth.

It's All About Attitude

I read a post the other day from a friend and pastor who talked about a family cancelling their Thanksgiving celebration this year, not over illness or fear of the pandemic, but over politics. I have personally watched a long-time friendship dissolve into a bitter and nasty rivalry, not over politics or a physical altercation, but over the effectiveness or lack thereof in wearing a mask.

 These were the thoughts in my mind as I looked at these pictures hanging on my living room wall. It brought a tear to my eye because I am watching the disintegration of family and friends unfold right in-front of me and I have no clue how to stop it.

And then God spoke…

"Why did you put the faith picture higher than the others?"

Because faith is more important.

"Why?"

Faith is the glue that holds the other two together.

"Do you really believe that?"

Yes.

"Then you know it's all about attitude, and you know what to do."

I had to ask myself, am I responding to what I see, or am I reacting. When I react, it comes from my emotions, but when I respond it comes from my experiential knowledge and the nudging of the Holy Spirit. My attitude shows the difference.

No matter what your political views are, or your feelings regarding the pandemic, or your religious beliefs, or the color of your skin, or your sexual preference... no matter what our differences or similarities are, you are welcome at my table.

You are welcome in my faith, family, and friends.

My prayer for me as well as the rest of the world is that we can let our attitude reflect love over bitterness. May we let our faith be a beacon of light in a dark and stormy world.

1 Corinthians 13:1-3
If I speak in the tongues of men or of angels, but do not have love, I am only a resounding gong or a clanging cymbal. If I have the gift of prophecy and can fathom all mysteries and all knowledge, and if I have a faith that can move mountains, but do not have love, I am nothing. If I give all I possess to the poor and give over my body to hardship that I may boast, but do not have love, I gain nothing.

God in our Pain

One of the hardest things I get asked as a pastor is some version of, "why does God allow pain?" It's usually when that person is either going through a storm or trying to decide if God is real. Explaining that God allows pain so that we learn to depend on Him and we can grow in our relationship with Him is so complicated because when you are in the middle of having your heart ripped out, the last thing you want to hear is that God will meet you in your pain. Everyone will tell you that you don't need to go through a storm to depend on God, they would always turn to God! He could do it differently!

I am really good about going to the dentist regularly. In the past I have had lots of dental issues due to a calcium deficiency, so I ensure that I have regular dental cleanings and let the dentist poke and prod as necessary. Prior to my last cleaning, I got the flu and had to cancel the appointment. I was sick enough that I didn't reschedule right then, I wanted to wait until I felt better.

Sunday, while at a birthday party, I broke one of the teeth out of my partial and had to call today to schedule an appointment to get it fixed. It has been 3 ½ years since my last dentist appointment. I forgot to call, and because I haven't had a problem with my teeth, it never crossed my mind to schedule a new appointment.

What would happen to our relationship with God if we didn't go through storms regularly? Would we forget to talk to Him? Out of sight out of mind?

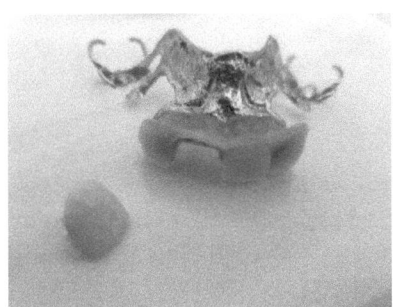

If we didn't need Him, how long before we forget He's always there for us? No pain, no problem right?

I know that as a result of other health issues I have to have regular dental cleanings, but I forgot it quickly.

I know that I need God daily digging into my junk! If He wasn't, I've shown how quickly I can forget. How about you?

Forgetting to schedule those dental appointments is going to cost me my front four teeth for two weeks. Lord help me to never know what would happen if I forgot You.

Let us NEVER forget!

Deuteronomy 4:9
Only be careful, and watch yourselves closely so that you do not forget the things your eyes have seen or let them fade from your heart as long as you live. Teach them to your children and to their children after them.

Greatest Need

Training Jake has been a difficult task to say the least. He is completely different from Tyler. Tyler is food driven, so all training  with him has revolved around his desire of snacks. Jake, however, is not food driven at all, he is play driven. He loves to be outdoors running around with sticks. If you use one to try to train him, he gets bored, runs off and finds another one to play with. I have had to change tactics more times than I care to count, and he still has a long way to go, as do I.

I was thinking about this as I prepared for last nights Flashcard Friday, Jesus' handling of two blind men in the Book of Mark. In Mark 8 Jesus spits in a man's eyes and then covers them with Hands twice, whereas in Mark 10 Jesus simply speaks and Bartimaeus receives the ability to see. Jesus met each of them in their greatest need and gave them what they wanted, in a way that they needed it the most. It was in all of this God reminded me that He meets each  and every one of us in our most important need, but not always in the way we prefer.

 For me that has meant putting on a muzzle and not always commenting when I really want to, not always responding when someone says something I strongly disagree with. It goes against my natural character not to say anything, and it's incredibly tough, but in it, God has taught me how to see His children in everyone I meet, even those I don't see eye to eye with. I have had to remind myself repeatedly that a person's true

character is revealed not in their response to those who they agree with, but those who they disagree with. But that's my road to travel. What is the journey God has for you?

All throughout Scripture, from Adam all the way to Zacchaeus, God meets each and every one of them in ways that teach not only them, but those around them, and He continues to do that with us today. It's not a punitive thing, it's a love thing. He wants what's best for us and is willing to teach us in a way that will get that point across to us and those around us.

It's likely going to be tough but walk it out anyway. Let His love heal those areas that have blinded you for too long.

1 Corinthians 12:21-26
The eye cannot say to the hand, "I don't need you!" And the head cannot say to the feet, "I don't need you!" On the contrary, those parts of the body that seem to be weaker are indispensable, and the parts that we think are less honorable we treat with special honor. And the parts that are unpresentable are treated with special modesty, while our presentable parts need no special treatment. But God has put the body together, giving greater honor to the parts that lacked it, so that there should be no division in the body, but that its parts should have equal concern for each other. If one part suffers, every part suffers with it; if one part is honored, every part rejoices with it.

Sun to Son

 When my husband's grandfather was still alive, his daughter planted three lilac bushes in the upper field. The two closest to each other were white and the one further away was a pale purple. Over the years the pale purple one sprouted shoots in the same area as one of the white bushes. The other day when I was walking the upper field with one of the dogs, I noticed that there are both purple and white blooms right next to each other. With all of the greenery surrounding the blooms, it looks like one plant with two different color blooms on it. Now when you dig in and look, it is two separate limbs, but they have actually intertwined with each other, so the blooms are side by side. It's absolutely beautiful to me.

As I was looking at the photos I took, it reminded me of the passage in Galatians 3:28 (NRSV), *"There is no longer Jew or Greek; there is no longer slave or free; there is no longer male and female, for all of you are one in Christ Jesus."*

Even though you and I see the differences between the blooms, they don't see it. Instead, they work together to reach the sun. I wonder what this world would be like if we all chose not to see the differences in each other, but rather worked together to reach the Son.

This world has gone so crazy that we've forgotten how to see beauty in all of God's creations. It is so easy to condemn, hate, and be afraid of anything that is different. It breaks my heart to see how we can claim to believe in a loving God with one hand and strike His creation with the other.

Maybe it is time to take a step back and do the hard work of reaching across the isle and locking arms with ALL of God's children no matter what they believe in. Maybe it's time for us to

open our eyes and look at the world with the lens that Jesus looks at us with.

Let's spread the Gospel with honey rather than arsenic.

IT IS TIME TO BE ONE IN CHRIST JESUS!

Tough Side of Growth

My husband and I have been renovating the upstairs bit by bit as we can afford it. Recent events have made it necessary to speed up the process in part of it. As we were organizing and going through stuff my husband came across a photo of a sonogram that was taken just before I miscarried. He wanted to know if I wanted to keep it and through tear filled eyes, I struggled to answer him. The pain cut like a knife straight  to my heart; it was eight years ago for you, but it was yesterday for me.

It was in that moment God whispered, "Don't stay there, look at what we've done."

Eight years ago, after three back-to-back miscarriages, a marriage in trouble, and chaos at work I wanted to give up. One minute I wanted to stay in bed forever, the next I wanted to find the nearest drug dealer, and the next I wanted to run away leaving all of the pain behind, but God... He held me tight, listened to me as I shook my fist at Him, patiently waiting for me to collapse in His loving arms. When my tears dried and my feeble strength returned, God and I went to work.

God showed me how to study His word and draw even closer than  before. He showed me how to move past my mistakes and save a beautiful marriage to a man I can't imagine being apart from. He walked me through my pride, my anger, and my selfish heart both at work and at home. The blessings He has shown me in the last eight years are too many to count.

He was faithful when I was faithless!

In her Bible Study on Job, author and speaker Lisa Harper wrote, "Often our greatest miracles are found on the other side of a river of tears." Those words speak straight to my heart and they are so true.

Yes, that loss will always be yesterday for me, but I know that it served as a launching point to bring me where I am today. I see the miracle of God each and every day, from my loving husband, to my "ride or die" friends, to the best co-workers on the planet, to the fact  that I can actually write this down. God has always been there; He is not done with my story yet...

And He's not done with your story either!

2 Timothy 2:11-13
Here is a trustworthy saying: If we died with him, we will also live with him; if we endure, we will also reign with him. If we disown him, he will also disown us; if we are faithless, he remains faithful, for he cannot disown himself.

Listen

Have you ever tried to create a list of things that needs to be done only to find that one thing requires something else to be done first which requires something else to be done first etc.? It's an overwhelming feeling isn't it? That has been my struggle lately at home. I have so many things that need to be cleaned, organized and/or repaired but one after another requires something else to be done 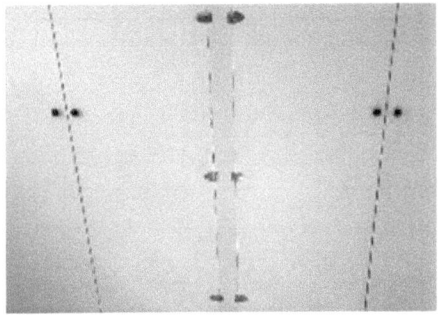 first. I was so overwhelmed looking at the list that I have spent days on the couch binge watching Netflix instead of getting started.

This may seem basic for most of you, but I have found that sometimes the most basic of things that we often forget the quickest. And God had to remind me of that very thing this week.

I know that I have lots of things to get done in the house, so on Tuesday night I asked some friends to pray for me to get busy. Because we were running late, when we got to the prayer request part of the evening, the decision was made to just use one or two words to describe what the prayer request was so that was all I said, "get busy" no details, no pity me party, no I'm so overwhelmed, it actually felt really good to do it that way. On my way home I turned the radio off, and just talked to God. I know that God has asked me to be still in other areas of my life, but this is one that I know I need to get busy doing and I needed His help. His response was simple, "just do ONE simple thing." My mind began to race, because, you know me, I can't do just one thing lol. So, the rest of the way home I started creating a list of several simple things I could get done on Wednesday. I knew that I didn't have any meetings, and Bob and I were only going to a movie that evening, so I had all day… or so I thought… Tell me you can hear God laughing!

When I got home, Bob had a message for me, my in-laws were going to breakfast the next morning and wondered if I would be interested in joining. I said yes, and then through more conversation with Bob decided to do the grocery shopping while I was out as well. By the time I got home, there was only a very short time to get anything done, and I could only do ONE thing. Yes, when you see the photos it's a dumb thing, but it was just what I needed to get started. Spending an hour changing out all of those knobs felt good; in my defense some of the original ones had to be broken off because they had been there too long. It has taken the overwhelming feeling out of the tasks I need to get done and actually made me excited to get more done. It also gave God some additional time to talk to me and remind me to really LISTEN to what He's saying.

We don't have to try to earn God's love by outdoing what He asks us to do. He gives freely to His children, and we could never earn it, we're not that good. What Jesus wants is simple, LISTEN and DO what He asks. Let His LOVE and GRACE wash over us daily as our relationship with Him deepens. Sometimes it's as easy as changing knobs on drawers and doors, but sometimes it's as hard as forgiving that person who hurt you deeply. It's WORTH it! So today I will simply say, "DO IT!" Whatever "it" is, there is a reason you are being asked, and Jesus is going to be right there with you, nudging, pushing, and carrying you all the way.

Mark 9:7
Then a cloud appeared and covered them, and a voice came from the cloud, "This is my Son, whom I love. Listen to him!"

The Danger in Distraction

This weekend was the start of our Holy Week that will culminate with the Easter Sunday celebration of our risen Jesus Christ. I was hoping to check out how churches around the world were beginning this celebration, yet when I opened up my social media feeds last night I was instead, greeted with the latest scandal in the entertainment world, a pair of shoes. Don't get me wrong, the shoes are completely disgusting, and I am saddened that they were even thought of  much less created. I even thought of writing my own condemnation of them, but something held me back.

A simple question from God…

"Why are you so easily distracted?"

Aren't you horrified by these shoes?

"I'm not worried about the shoes; I'm worried about you."

What do you mean?

"This week is the celebration of the fulfillment of a promise. A gift to end the separation of Myself from My children, and a debt My Son gave His life to pay for. You let a pair of shoes turn your attention away from that! Do you see the danger in those kinds of distractions? What should you really be doing right now?"

As usual God's words are right on target. I let something small distract me from the celebration of the one true King, the only King for me. It could have easily swept me in and carried me down the river of anger and outrage in a week that should be filled with the waters of prayer and thanksgiving. My hands were fisted at my side instead of waving in the air. Not this week satan!

It wasn't by accident that word of this distraction hit social media just prior to Palm Sunday. It wasn't by accident the shoes were released today along with the corresponding and equally horrible song. The enemy of our souls picked a time that would most enrage us to distract us from the wonders and glory of a God who gave up His very life for us.

When the disciples asked Jesus who is the greatest in the kingdom  of Heaven, he pulled a child to him and said that unless they became like children, they would never enter heaven (Matthew 18:1-5). He spun their distraction of which one was better than the other to the thing that mattered most, following Jesus. The child in this passage came willingly to Jesus. They didn't fuss or get distracted; they simply did as Jesus asked. And what is the biggest action God calls us to? What's that thing I should be doing instead of being distracted? Prayer.

Instead of spending my time in my distraction I should be walking my neighborhood praying over each and every home that I walk by. Praying that, as Passover approaches, they are kept safe from the enemy and all of his distractions. I should be thanking my Savior for a gift that I will never be able to fully fathom. A gift that only He could give, and one that saved my very soul.

I don't know about you, but my dogs and I need to go for a quiet prayerful walk around a few blocks.

Galatians 5:13-14
You, my brothers and sisters, were called to be free. But do not use your freedom to indulge the flesh; rather, serve one another humbly in love. For the entire law is fulfilled in keeping this one command: "Love your neighbor as yourself."

All Things New

Rainy days and a nasty summer cold have limited my mowing time this season. I was super happy to see that there was no rain in the forecast and the temperatures were perfect for an afternoon of God time on my mower, and He did not disappoint! From the moment the mower blades lowered He spoke; there were tears, and there was laughter, and it was all so very needed.

Both personally as well as professionally I am in a season of change. The ups and downs that come with all of this change are a little rough to travel through. I've been trying to find my rhythm in the midst of all the chaos, but if I'm honest, I feel a little like a hamster running in the wheel to nowhere. Hearing God's voice so loud and clear today is beyond a welcome surprise.

One of the first images He blessed me with was a monarch butterfly down by the lake. As I shed a tear at the absolute beauty of this creature I could hear God whisper, "Behold, I make all things new."

Why does it have to hurt so much? You know I don't like change, and it feels like you're changing everything! It's hard to breathe through this whirl wind of upheaval.

"Baby, those are growing pains. In many ways you are like that butterfly of Mine you were just admiring. As a caterpillar you ran from me seeking only the things of this world and it almost broke you. When I found you beaten and bruised, I wrapped you in the chrysalis of My love. I taught, and you studied and learned. Now it's time for you to break through that cocoon and learn to fly with the new wings I have given you."

Why does it feel like it's all happening at once?

"The muscles we have been building are ready to work, but for that to happen I need you focused on me. When menopause brings feelings of loss, look to Me. When it brings feelings of release, look to Me. When the chaos in your job leaves you confused, look to Me. When it brings feelings of pure joy, look to Me. Behold, I am making all things new!"

The work of God in my life is the most amazing thing to see as I look back over 53 years, but the last two years God has completely shocked and overwhelmed me with blessings. The study and writing have been so intense, often leaving me with days that my brain  was so overworked I could barely function. The culmination of all that study has come in the way of a Bible study. Writing this has taught me to continually keep my gaze focused on Jesus. It was a journey of love and God was faithful to walk with me through every up and down and every twist and turn.

My day on the mower reminded me that God is ALWAYS making things new, in my life... and yours. HE LOVES YOU and He is walking with you through whatever chaos life has thrown your way! He is your protector whether you are in a caterpillar season, chrysalis season. He's even there when it is time for you to FLY!

Isaiah 40:29-31
He gives strength to the weary and increases the power of the weak. Even youths grow tired and weary, and young men stumble and fall; but those who hope in the Lord will renew their strength. They will soar on wings like eagles; they will run and not grow weary, they will walk and not be faint.

Softened Heart

Today is an unusual day for me to be writing a devotional. There is a funeral for a family member today and it's September 11th, a day this nation will remember forever. This is a day when we need to be quiet and reflective about the gifts we have been given and somberly remembering those who lost their lives on a day when our great country was attacked. What could God possibly be wanting to teach me today?

"You have spent over a year studying My Son and how He is found in the Old Testament, what have you learned?"

Wow, I've learned so much! Jesus is all over the Old Testament, from Genesis to Malachi, from prophesy to physical form, the Old Testament is about Him.

"That's head knowledge, what have YOU learned?"

That the Old Testament is an outline of my relationship with you. The ups and downs, the joys, and the tears; it's all written in those pages. I have changed both for good and bad, but you never have. You have stayed true and have been faithful throughout.

"The last thing you've studied so far is Balaam's story, did it soften your heart?"

I hope so, that's been my prayer since I started reading his story.

"If that's been your prayer, then why don't you know it to be true."

Because I still struggle trusting you.

"Why? If I'm as faithful as you claim to believe, why don't you trust Me?"

Because there are moments when I think you only saved me because you felt sorry for me. There are moments when I think you've lost your mind for choosing me to do anything. In those moments I can't see your faithfulness.

"Stop."

It's not that easy.

"Yes, it is, I saved you because I love you. I chose you because you are my child. That will never change."

Following God is not an easy road to travel; it takes a faith that is impossible to explain or understand. If you are anything like me, you will stumble and fall routinely. Every time conviction shows a hard spot on our hearts, we need to be open to the working of the Holy Spirit and let Him soften the rough edges of our comfortability. We need to trust that God will not leave us there, that He is faithful and never changes.

GOD LOVES YOU! GOD CHOSE YOU! YOU ARE HIS!

You only have to BELIEVE.

Psalm 33:10-11
The Lord foils the plans of the nations; he thwarts the purposes of the peoples. But the plans of the Lord stand firm forever, the purposes of his heart through all generations.

Willing to do the Work

I can grow most outside plants without a problem, you could almost say I have a green thumb. Move those plants inside and that green thumb quickly turns black. Keeping plants alive inside is not my forte to say the least. I have killed both a cactus and an aloe vera plant; two of the easiest to keep alive.

 Last year, when I got a new job, a friend brought me an indoor plant to celebrate the occasion. I was crying inside because I just knew I was going to kill it. It's an African violet, a very temperamental plant and hard to keep alive. Another trusted friend gave me some tips, so I determined to change my title from killer to grower. As an added test, I set out to keep a beautiful dark red geranium that my mother-in-law bought me alive throughout the winter as well.

I learned about watering from the bottom, removing dust off the leaves with a soft brush, and paying attention to the amount of light each plant got. I was and continue to be diligent in caring for each of them they way they are supposed to be. There was a moment in late Spring that both of them looked pretty rough and I thought I was going to lose each of them, but I pressed on and continued to do what I had read and learned. It didn't take much, just a few minutes a week, but what it did require was intentionality on my part.

Miraculously, they are both thriving and BLOOMING over a year later! In my excitement over this God spoke…

"With intentionality we can do beautiful things."

It's hard sometimes.

"Yes, I know, but the willingness to do the work produces a strength you never thought possible. And that strength produces the most beautiful of blooms."

There are days when focusing on my relationship with God is hard. Those times when I feel let down, or pushed too far, times when I just want that momentary break. That's when I have to press on and continue to do the work. When I do that, I blossom into the woman He's nurturing me to be.

I know it seems pointless at times. I know it hurts. I know you want to quit fighting. I know that being vulnerable sucks sometimes. It's in that storm that God builds our strength.

Because HE KNOWS the point of our story. HE KNOWS the muscles we build through the pain. HE KNOWS the drive we have to succeed. HE KNOWS the value of our untethered honesty. HE KNOWS the flower that blooms after the rain.

DON'T QUIT... HE KNOWS... HE CARES... HE LOVES... YOU!

Romans 5:1-5
Therefore, since we have been justified through faith, we have peace with God through our Lord Jesus Christ, through whom we have gained access by faith into this grace in which we now stand. And we boast in the hope of the glory of God. Not only so, but we also glory in our sufferings, because we know that suffering produces perseverance; perseverance, character; and character, hope. And hope does not put us to shame, because God's love has been poured out into our hearts through the Holy Spirit, who has been given to us.

Secure in the Father's Love

Jake was taken from his mother at three weeks, so he didn't get some of the necessary training and security the mom provides in the first weeks of life. As a result of this, he's pretty skittish. He doesn't like loud noises, thunderstorms, or being outside at night when he can't see what's beyond the lights. Any unusual noise while he's outside and he's running for the front door fighting to get inside. He is getting better, but we know that it will take quite some time for him to overcome this.

When we first picked Jake up from the shelter he spent the majority

 of the time with me, going to work and meetings with me, sleeping on my lap while I tried to write and study at home. Bob's job had him in Ann Arbor all day during the week, and weekends he was working outside, so it was completely expected when Jake chose me to be his human. It was also fully expected that Jake really didn't do much with Bob as he just wasn't there a lot and Jake didn't trust him.

Enter, Covid-19 and a global pandemic. Because Bob now works from home it made more sense to leave Jake with him when I went to work at the church or had meetings around town. He goes with me every now and then, but we discovered that he is way more comfortable at home with Bob and our other dog, Tyler. Now that Bob takes him outside, makes sure he has food and water, Jake now trusts him and feels secure when he's around; so secure that he will even sleep on top of Bob's foot.

It was in this moment that God spoke...

"Are you that secure in My Love?"

Yes

"Are you sure?"

I may have a moment here and there when I'm not as secure.

"Why is that?"

Sometimes it feels like you put me in situations, and people say or do things that hurt, and it makes me doubt Your protection.

"Those are the situations I want you to feel the most secure. It's not you they are attacking, it's the light of Me shining through you that they fight against. I've got your back and your front, if you will only step back and let Me absorb the blow. Baby, that's how deep My love for you is."

There's a saying floating around social media lately, "When we feel the stress of the storm, we learn the strength of our anchor." This is so true! My head knows that most of the time people are lashing out at the God they see in me, but I have to fight to get my heart to fully understand that. God loves us so much that we can feel safe and secure with Him.

We can even be completely secure sleeping at His feet.

BELIEVE IN THE SECURITY OF HIS LOVE

Hebrews 6:18-19
God did this so that, by two unchangeable things in which it is impossible for God to lie, we who have fled to take hold of the hope set before us may be greatly encouraged. We have this hope as an anchor for the soul, firm and secure. It enters the inner sanctuary behind the curtain.

Double Scoop

Normally they are not allowed on the bed, but they wanted me out of it WAY too soon this morning, so I broke my own rule and let  them up. Two hours later I woke up to find that my back, from my neck to my ankles was on fire. I turned my head to find two dogs spooning and pressed up against me on one side, and I was so close to the edge on the other side that I could count the carpet fibers. My only escape would be to use the wall to balance myself to prevent falling flat on my face on the floor.

And the God spoke…

"What would happen if you rolled over instead of getting out of bed?"

It would be next to impossible, and there would definitely be a wrestling match involved, but the boys would love a little play time.

"That's what our relationship is like. Sometimes it's hard, and we wrestle our way through, but I LOVE spending time with you. You're WORTH every twist and turn we go through."

Having a Heavenly Father willing to go through what He must go through with me is mind boggling. I can be stubborn, and pig headed, and I'm definitely a mistake prone windbag, but God is with me each and every moment. His grace and and love has brought me through more than I could ever ask or imagine. I can say without a doubt that I have never seen His receding back.

To each and every one of us He brings a LOVE that knows no bounds, and FORGIVENESS that we could never earn on our own power. He Loves us right where we are, and He refuses to leave us where we are. He routinely pushes us to more and better. Yes it's hard, and sometimes we/I wrestle with what He's asking, but in the end I know that what He wants is ALWAYS best.

TRUST THE ONE WHO LOVED YOU FIRST!

P.S. Tyler and Jake loved the playtime this morning.

Deuteronomy 31:6
Be strong and courageous. Do not be afraid or terrified because of them, for the Lord your God goes with you; he will never leave you nor forsake you."

GOT RECOVERY?

Last week I was having some trouble and found myself a little dizzy with a mild headache. I had just recently come back from vacation where not only did I stay at a much higher altitude than Michigan, but I also spent several hours on a plane. That coupled with a high pollen count has my sinuses all out of whack and I was pretty sure that was the reason for my difficulties. So, I was talking to my sister-in-law about it and knowing that I prefer natural remedies over medications she recommended a supplement for me to try. I purchased it the following morning and started taking it right away. Within 24 hours the supplement started to work. I had junk coming out of my eyes, nose, ears, and throat, and my mild headache had turned into a raging thump inside my brain. Needless to say, I was not happy! I had a little dizziness and a tiny headache, and now I can barely move off the couch and my sinuses are draining everywhere! I was content in my minor ailment, but I was miserable in my recovery process.

That seems to be a natural trend for us. In the book of John there is a paralytic man sitting by a pool. He knows that if he can just get into that pool he could be healed, but for 38 years he waited on the sidelines. Then Jesus walks up to him and asks a simple question, "Do you want to get well?" Instead of saying yes, the man proceeds to give Jesus a list of reasons he hasn't been healed up to this point. I wonder, was he afraid of the pain of recovery? Was that fear what was keeping him from the pool? I think it was. I think the pain of recovery was too scary for him and so he waited. Is that what you are doing? Is fear holding you back? Jesus is saying the same thing to us that He said to that man after he gave his list of excuses, "Get up! Pick up your mat and walk."

I know it's scary, I know recovery is going to be uncomfortable and it's going to hurt, but I am living proof that it's worth the fear and pain. If God would choose to stand by me as I recovered from addiction, abuse, emotional turmoil, and even overactive sinuses, He will absolutely stand by you. Do you want to get well?

Author and Christian speaker Christine Caine shares often of her recovery following knee surgery. Her physical therapist told her that her right knee was now stronger than it was before, but to get it to function properly again was going to take some pain. She could just learn to walk again and nothing more, or she could fully recover all function out of her knee. The degree to which she was willing to embrace the pain of recovery was the degree to which she would recover. She fought through the pain and chose to fully recover. Do you want to fully recover? Are you willing to embrace the pain of recovery?

A week later, my sinuses are finally starting to clear, I got up this morning to a dull roar of a headache, the dizziness is gone, and there is no more drainage. I was wandering around the house thanking God for helping me through this and walked into my prayer room to the coolest "you're welcome" from God. My favorite bird is a barn swallow, I think they are just so beautiful, and I love it when they gracefully fly in front of the lawnmower snatching up the bugs that the mower has scared into flight. I usually only see two or three flying around, but this morning as I gazed out the window overlooking the upper field, there was probably twenty or thirty of them flying around. Some of them even buzzed the window I was standing by. Talk about a Jesus hug!

Jesus is willing to walk with us through the pain of recovery and love us step by step. He knows our pain, but He knows what waits on the other side of the pain. Author and Christian speaker Lisa Harper wrote, "sometimes our greatest miracles lie on the other side of a river of tears." Don't miss out on your miracle! Embrace the pain of recovery with your eyes fixed on Jesus! He won't ever leave you!

John 5:6

When Jesus saw him there and learned that he had been in this condition for a long time, he asked him, "Do you want to get well?"

LIVING INTENTIONAL

This week was another crazy week for me. I am beginning to think that this is my new normal lol because every time I think "if I can  just get past this, life will go back to normal," then something else brings chaos to my world and I say those words again. So, either chaos is my normal or normal is a mythical unicorn... I just don't know lol.

Living with all of this recent chaos, I am learning the true meaning of intentionality. I was reading an Instragram devotional from Lisa Harper this afternoon, and she has the same difficulty saying no that I do. She has been faced with a decision, one that I am facing as well; either learn to say "no" with regularity or learn to be intentional with the smaller moments of peace and quiet that you have. Like Miss Harper, I say no from time to time, but if I can fit something into my schedule, I am more likely to say yes. As a result, I am having to learn how to be VERY intentional with the fewer moments of quiet that I have.

I love watching storms roll in over the lake, and God has been showing off the beauty of a storm rolling in the past couple of weeks. The clouds have just been gorgeous, and the way the lightening lights them up, it's just amazing! I may only get a half an hour here and there, but I am loving learning how to be intentional with those moments, and God has been so faithful in helping me to not only see it but appreciate it as well. I LOVE

getting to do ALL the things I do, even when it completely exhausts me but even more, I LOVE it when God goes out of His way just to make me smile; when He gives me His peace, there is NO BETTER feeling on the planet!

John 14:27
Peace I leave with you; my peace I give you. I do not give to you as the world gives. Do not let your hearts be troubled and do not be afraid.

Trapped in the Cage of Too Much

Meet Jake's new buddy Chippie!

 With my husband working from home for the foreseeable future he decided to put a few bird feeders outside his office window. One of our resident chipmunks has decided that he will help himself to this delectable treat on a regular basis and Jake just loves to watch him from the window and then race around to the feeder when we let him out only to find his friend long gone.

Chippie faces a dilemma however when he's stuffed his cheeks full with food to take home to his family... he can no longer squeeze through the cage of the feeder and he has to make a choice. He can swallow the food and have nothing to take home, or he can spit it out on the ground and try to get down to it before the mourning doves and European starlings snatch it all up. Watching all of this unfold can be quite entertaining! I found myself watching the other day when God spoke...

"Can you see yourself in this little chipmunk?"

What do you mean?

"If he took just a small amount of food, he could easily traverse back and forth between the bars. Instead, he overstuffs himself and can no longer do what he set out to do. You, and so many more of my children take on too much and as a result, can no longer do what you were sent out to do."

It's hard to know when I've taken on too much, it's all good things, and they all glorify You.

49

"Think about those moments when you are running so hard you don't have time to stop and think. Those moments when the chaos overwhelms you and you cut your finger while making lunch for your husband. Those moments when your mind won't shut off and you can't get any sleep. I've called you to some difficult arenas that will require you to rely solely on Me, so I need you to trust Me when I tell you to say no to really good things. I need you to trust that I have someone else for that job."

It's really hard to get caught up in all of the good things we get to do as Christian brothers and sisters, but are we going beyond what  God has called us to do? I am learning to ask myself an incredibly difficult question, "am I preventing someone else from finding their calling?" I know the arenas God has called me to, and I know that they take up a lot of my time. It forces me to use a two-letter word that doesn't roll off my tongue very easy, "no." Sometimes us saying no allows someone else to say yes, and in that they find where God is calling them.

Balance is not a mythical unicorn like I used to think. Balance is focusing on Jesus and following His lead, it's finding Him in the midst of the chaos we create and saying no to really good things and trusting that He has the right person at the right time. Sounds simple, I know, but trust me when I say it's harder than we all think.

TRUST in the One who loves us beyond what we can comprehend.

Proverbs 16:20
Whoever gives heed to instruction prospers, and blessed is the one who trusts in the Lord.

A Lesson In Patience

Jake has been struggling with a shoulder injury for a few months

now. It gets better and then he re-injures it and we have to start the healing process all over again. The vet had us try a medication to keep him calm, but it had the reverse effect and hyped him up. We don't want to use the stronger medications because of the side effects so we do our best to keep him quiet when his shoulder is in need of a break, but it's hard for him. He's barely a year old, and he's super active.

Being a puppy, his favorite game is still fetch. Inside he has a ball that he will keep bringing until your arm feels like it's going to fall off. Outside it consists of me throwing a stick and watching him run around with it in his mouth until he tires out. When his shoulder is acting up, we can't do these activities and he goes bonkers, begging for a little activity. Patience is not something he aspires to at all!

So today when he got to go outside for the first time in five days he was beyond excited. I managed to capture his expression as he impatiently waited for me to throw his beloved stick, and when I did it was like he had been shot out of a cannon. He raced all over the yard with it in his mouth just as happy as can be. We came inside, he drank the water bowl dry, we massaged his shoulder, and then he curled up like a pretzel in the chair and went right to sleep.

As I looked back on our morning activities God spoke…

"Jake's lack of patience looks a lot like yours."

What do you mean?

"With almost everything in your life you push and push until you get the okay and then you race through it so fast that you wear yourself out. Being forced to move slowly and patiently as you continue to write that Bible study, has you so antsy at times you lose focus. What you haven't realized yet is that if you would continue to be patient you would enjoy life so much more. There are blessings around every corner for all of my children, you just have to slow down and see it!"

 As we move through this journey with Christ, we have to remember that it's God who determines our steps. He has things for us to see and experience all of the time, but if we are always racing toward the next best thing, we miss out on the daily multitude of blessings He has for us.

Jake plays hard and sleeps hard, he winds up in positions that just don't look comfortable. It works for him, but as I look at my life and the crazy Jesus journey I'm walking, Jake's way won't work for me; I would miss out on too much.

Stop racing and relish all that God has placed in front of you. Feel the blessings found in your relationship with your Creator Redeemer.

ENJOY all of the little MOMENTS!

Colossians 3:12-14
Therefore, as God's chosen people, holy and dearly loved, clothe yourselves with compassion, kindness, humility, gentleness and patience. Bear with each other and forgive one another if any of you has a grievance against someone. Forgive as the Lord forgave you. And over all these virtues put on love, which binds them all together in perfect unity.

Changing One

God and I have been having a lot of conversations lately, and today

was no exception. Between the flashcard Friday teachings and writing in my Bible study, I have been spending the majority of my Bible time in the Old Testament. Then this morning I made the mistake of looking at the news; side note, don't ever do that when you're in a mood. When I finished, I think my brain literally exploded! Over three thousand years later and, WE STILL HAVE NOT LEARNED!

Politics, oppression, racism, sexual and gender identity, etc., ALL of the things we are fighting about today can be found in Genesis through Malachi, and again in Matthew through Revelation. As I have scoured through maps, teachings, studies, sermons looking at what people went through in the Old and New Testament, I am finding that it is a MIRROR of what we are facing today.

In the spirit of honesty, I felt defeated and beaten. With the wind

knocked completely out of my sails, my prayer was simple, God what are we doing? What's the point of standing in the gap you have placed me in? History shows we are incapable of learning, Your Word shows we are incapable of learning. Why am I allowing myself to be

wounded repeatedly over a situation we haven't learned from in all this time?

His words were simple, sweet, and to the point…

"Shh, lean into my chest and breathe, I've got you. A hundred years passed between Jonah and Nahum; how many generations were saved as a result of Jonah being used by Me to speak to the

Ninevites? Over 500 years passed between Esther and Matthew; how many generations were saved as a result of her willingness to stand? Many repented and turned toward Me. On the outside it looks like nothing changed, but there are more in My Kingdom as a result of a single person willing to stand in a gap. How many generations will learn because of what you and I are doing? I'm not asking you to change the world, I'm asking you to change YOU. Esther and Jonah didn't change the world, they changed; they moved closer to Me. People saw the changes IN THEM more than they heard the words coming out of their mouths. That my sweet daughter is the point."

When you stand in a gap, people will mock and throw stones, but God is the deflector shield that others should see. Friends and family will walk away, so learn to lean in like John into the chest of Jesus and let the calmness of His breathing be your comfort in the emotional storm. Study, learn, lean, speak, but most importantly change.

Let the change in YOU be the loudest voice in the gap!

Romans 5:15
But the gift is not like the trespass. For if the many died by the trespass of the one man, how much more did God's grace and the gift that came by the grace of the one man, Jesus Christ, overflow to the many!

Worry About You

A few weeks ago, I had an awesome conversation with a family member and learned that we are both being taught the same lesson from God. I just love those moments when you find out that you are not alone, and that God loves us all so much that He will teach the same lesson over and over again until we ALL get it.

I was thinking about that today as I was mowing. Now that the buckhorn is under control it's time to switch from mowing at 3

inches to 2 inches. It can be tricky in the lower field because the grass is thicker, there are multiple angles, trees and shrubs to combat mow around, and with the lake level so high, it's still soggy in spots. Because of the wetness you have to keep the mower moving to prevent the wheels from digging in and getting stuck (I may have done that a time or two over the years lol), but you also have to speed up and slow down depending on the thickness of the grass. I never knew you had to be a mathematician just to mow a lawn!

I had all of this twisting through my head (yes, I know I have issues lol) when God spoke...

"Your husband has mowed this lawn since he was a small child. As a result, he knows each and every twist and turn. He knows how to maneuver the high and low spots, the trees and bushes, and how to keep from overturning the mower on the steep angled areas. Am I right?"

Yes

"Why does he trust you to mow this area now?"

Because he taught me how to do it.

"Do you ever mess up?"

Yes, all the time.

"Why does he still trust you?"

Because each time I make a mistake, he teaches me how to overcome it and prevent it from happening in the future, sometimes he has to reiterate points, but we make a pretty good team.

"That's what our relationship is like. I'm teaching you how to move in your lane. When you make a mistake, I teach you how to overcome it and prevent it from happening again, even if it takes multiple tries, I think you and I make a pretty good team as well."

I think that too

"Then trust me to do that with others as well. You stay focused on our relationship and building that. Let me worry about all of my other children."

His words are so true for each and every one of us. It's easy to get caught up in what you neighbor is doing wrong. It's easy to point fingers at the other political party, or a friend's decision on vaccinations. It's easy to throw words around like "sheeple," or "socialist," or "racist," or even "cancel culturist." It's hard to let others have their own opinions and make their own decisions. It's even harder to focus solely on the lessons God has laid before us. To learn from our own

mistakes and lean in on God when we don't think we can take another step.

But the hardest thing of all… trust God with others.

It's tough to realize that WE are NOT the savior of the world, HE IS. But it's true! He does a way better job than we ever could, and here's the really funny thing… all of "those people" who don't listen to you… they LISTEN TO HIM.

I'm choosing to worry about my relationship with God. I'm also choosing to trust Him with you.

Psalm 20:6-7
Now this I know: The Lord gives victory to his anointed. He answers him from his heavenly sanctuary with the victorious power of his right hand. Some trust in chariots and some in horses, but we trust in the name of the Lord our God.

I Am With You Always

Somewhere around January I entered into menopause, and it has been quite a journey. My doctor had let me know a head of time  that women who have never given birth tend to have a few · more obstacles than those who have been blessed with a biological child. As she predicted I started noticing that my highs and lows were skewing to extremes. I shared this with a trusted friend, and they routinely remind me that this is hormones, or the lack there of, and that I'm not losing my mind. It has helped tremendously having her guide me through, but if I'm being honest, sometimes I wonder.

Today was my first opportunity to mow the lower field and get a little God time, so I got all dressed and ready, had my music going, and the lawnmower wouldn't start. I could feel my temperature rising, but using the breathing techniques I have learned, I brought it back down pretty quick. A few more attempts and tricks, and it finally started, phew, I knew I needed this God time. Then my phone decides to have the music cut in and out; the songs are downloaded, this shouldn't happen! Typically, I would just turn off the tunes and let God speak to me in a different way, but menopause kicked in, and I let the music play, all while getting madder and madder as the songs continued to skip and break. At one point I even thought of throwing my phone into the lake just to show it how I felt.

When the music cut out of a really good song, I stopped the lawnmower, my face beat red with anger, ready to scream, a still small voice called out…

"Baby, I'm with you in this storm, breathe and know that I've got you. You are not alone, and this will pass; lean in and breathe."

At the sound of His voice, I could feel my muscles begin to release the tension that had been building; my heart began to beat a little slower, and with a simple whisper and a gentle Hand my spirit settled down and the much-needed tears began to flow. Menopause and the knowledge that I will never have a child slowly began to release and I could finally breathe in the glorious sounds of God's gentle words.

I don't know what storm you are currently walking through, but I know that you are not alone. Listen to the whispers of a God who cares, a God who has never left your side, and a God who will never show you His back.

Breathe my friend! Breathe in the Glory of the Most High and let His Spirit fill you with hope and peace.

God loves you… and so do I!

Isaiah 43:2
When you pass through the waters, I will be with you; and when you pass through the rivers, they will not sweep over you. When you walk through the fire, you will not be burned; the flames will not set you ablaze.

How Deep Are You Willing To Go?

This devotional is going to be quite different from any that I have ever done. If I'm being honest, I might not even have the courage to post it lol.

Last week I read a blog based on a Scripture in 1 Peter, and it made me mad on some levels and flat ticked me off on other levels. Take a look at the Scripture, and then we'll talk... *1 Peter 3:1-6 'Wives, in the same way submit yourselves to your own husbands so that, if any of them do not believe the word, they may be won over without words by the behavior of their wives, when they see the purity and reverence of your lives. Your beauty should not come from outward adornment, such as elaborate hairstyles and the wearing of gold jewelry or fine clothes. Rather, it should be that of your inner self, the unfading beauty of a gentle and quiet spirit, which is of great worth in God's sight. For this is the way the holy women of the past who put their hope in God used to adorn themselves. They submitted themselves to their own husbands, like Sarah, who obeyed Abraham and called him her lord. You are her daughters if you do what is right and do not give way to fear.'*

The blog writer focused on the literal aspect of two things in this passage: women should not wear jewelry and should obey their husbands the way Sarah did. While the author is technically right, I struggled with what was missing. If you are going to focus on the literal wording, it's my personal opinion that you have to take the whole passage and not "cherry pick" what you want to focus on. When you take the passage as a whole, you see that Peter is talking to gentile women who are new to the faith and their husbands do not believe in God. He's telling them that their behavior is what will win their husbands over, not their beauty and not their words. It's actually a very tender and loving moment that Peter is sharing here and not a dictating "do what you're told" moment. Please don't take my word for it. Study this passage for yourself, read the commentaries, listen to the many sermons on it. It's an amazing text!

I got past that irritation really quick because doubt was creeping in. You see, the author has a master's degree in theology, and I don't. Who am I to question someone so learned? Two people that I trust explicitly helped me walk through that pretty quickly as well. As God planned it, they both said the same exact words to me, "you don't have to have a degree to study the Bible." It seems simple as I look at it written on this page, but when you have an ongoing battle with your self-esteem, it's a mountain to climb over. It's really easy for me to climb inside my turtle shell because I see someone as "better" or "smarter" than me. Thankfully God has placed people in my life that don't let me sit in that pity party too long.

You would think that by the time I climbed through all of that I would be done with this blog and this passage. But God had other plans for me. In the last two years I have been learning to look beyond the literal wording of Scripture and to search for the beautiful gems (pun intended) hidden underneath the wording. The gem underneath this passage is LIFE CHANGING!

When I read the passage for the five hundredth time, two words jumped out: adorn and sight. Adorn means to "put on" or "wrap yourself in" and sight means to "focus on" or "see." What was it that Sarah saw? When you travel back to the book of Genesis you find that Sarah's story starts in chapter 11, her name was Sarai, and God would later change it to Sarah, the mother of all nations. She was a very beautiful and wealthy woman; she could have had anything she wanted. But in that day and age if a beautiful woman was noticed by other men, they would kill the husband in order to marry the woman. Sarah was not afraid of her husband, she loved him deeply, so she went out of her way to NOT be noticed, she didn't wear fine clothes, jewelry, or braid her hair, or speak loudly in public. She "put on" a quiet and reverent spirit in a desire to protect and love her husband. Her "focus," her desire, her HEART was for Abraham.

Jesus tells us throughout that ALL Scripture is ultimately about Him and our relationship with Him. Now look at the passage through that lens. Jesus, through Peter, is telling us to FOCUS on Him. It's not about your hair, your jewelry, or even your clothing. It's about getting up every morning saying, "Jesus, change me from the inside out. Set my selfish desires and childish fears aside. Help me see other's the way You do, help me love them as You do. Clothe me in your righteousness so that the world can see Your light." Next time you look at that person who annoys you the most, look beneath the mask of protection they wear and see the beauty within. Don't notice them, SEE Jesus in them.

That passage is about a HEART change and a FOCUS change. Set your sight on Jesus and adorn your heart with His love. That's what I see when I read those words. What do you see?

John 5:39
You study the Scriptures diligently because you think that in them you have eternal life. These are the very Scriptures that testify about me."

Friendship

As predicted Jake and Tyler are starting to develop quite the friendship. When we first brought Jake home Tyler did everything

he could to push him away. Now when Jake is off somewhere with one of us Tyler waits impatiently by the door for his return. They used to sleep in different areas in the living room and now they can usually be found side by side. Tyler has begun to teach Jake what it means to be a dog, from defending himself to loving the humans who take care of him. Jake is soaking it all up and loving every minute of it. Even when they argue, there is a sense of loyalty between the two of them, an unbreakable bond of brothers.

Watching the relationship between these two develop brought to mind Jesus and His disciples. They started off wary of Jesus at first, questioning and testing everything. But by the end, trust had been established and they learned daily as He taught them all they would need to know about being His disciple. They still made mistakes, and they bickered from time to time, but the bond had been established on a solid foundation.

Isn't that what Jesus is asking of us? Isn't that the relationship He wants with us?

Learning from the teaching of His Word and reaching for Him before we react in ANY situation is what He's asking of each and every one of us. I, like many of you wrestle with this notion from time to time. He let's me stumble and fall, but I can honestly say, He is the first one to reach down, pick me up, and dust me off. He has never failed me, and He will never fail you.

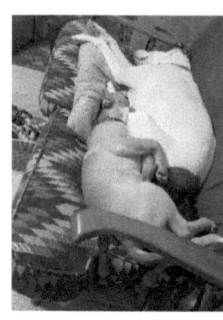

Put your trust in the FRIEND who sticks closer than a BROTHER!

You won't be disappointed!

John 8:12
When Jesus spoke again to the people, he said, "I am the light of the world. Whoever follows me will never walk in darkness, but will have the light of life."

Seasons

One of the most common things you hear when you are going through a difficult time is, "hang on, this is just a season." I even say it myself quite often. It's a true statement and there is some comfort in it, but if I'm honest it can be hard to hear at times. Why is that? Maybe it feels like it minimizes the pain, or maybe it's just because we want this season to finally end.

See I've gone through and am still going through multiple seasons at one time. I have two dogs, one old and one young, who are each walking through different fairly severe health issues that force me to do medications for each at different times. I finished writing and publishing a Bible study and was excited to begin the next one when my friend and boss moved out of the country which left the church I work at in a time of transition that prevented me from writing for an extended "season." I have a new boss now and he is an absolute pleasure to work with, so I'm finding that writing just

might be a possibility again which is super exciting, but where do I start? Fall has finally given way to winter and that changes my at home cleaning and cooking responsibilities which became weirdly complicated when I came down with a very mild case of Covid. I'm feeling a gentle nudge to start taking some online theology classes, and I'm also feeling a nudge to teach a class as well. Can you see all these seasons lol?

I have no doubt if you were to take a moment and list yours out you would find that you have just as many if not more than I do. So how do you feel when people say, "it's just a season?"

As I searched the Scriptures for guidance, I found that depending on the version, "season" is found multiple times. The obvious draw would be Ecclesiastes 3 and the "there is a season for everything

under the sun," passage. I found myself drawn, however, to Psalm 104. This one is loosely attributed to David, but as it's not titled, the authorship of Psalm 104 is actually unknown. What I like about it, and what makes it apropos for me is that the author uses what he sees in nature to praise God for all of the seasons of life we face.

From verses 19 to 23, the author shows the necessity of both moon and sun, some things hunt during the day and some at night. Theologian Adam Clarke says it best, "And as it would not be convenient for man and the wild beasts of the forest to collect their food at the same time, he has given the night to them as the proper time to procure their prey, and the day to rest in. When MAN labors, THEY rest; when MAN rests, THEY labor." Now don't get me wrong, I don't think God creates our tough seasons, I believe He allows them based on our good and bad decisions.

As I'm going through a tough season, others are going through fun and exciting times. In this we can encourage each other and lift each other up. Seeing other friends going through high points is exciting for me when I'm in a valley because I know that my mountain top experience is coming, all I have to do is keep my head up and focused on God during the rough spots. He is always faithful to walk with me through the darkest moments!

GOD IS FAITHFUL!
BELIEVE IT!
HE WILL NOT LEAVE YOU!

Psalm 104:19
He made the moon to mark the seasons; the sun knows its time for setting.

Still Standing

I was blessed recently to spend time with my friend and mentor. While waiting outside, I found myself enamored with this basketball net. Her children have grown and moved away, so it's been some time since this net has seen any use and it's looking pretty weathered. What's wild is that while the backboard and pole are marred and scarred up and the metal netting is pretty well rusted, it all stands straight and tall.

And then God spoke…

"What do you see when you look at this?"

I see a basketball net that has seen its better days.

"You're looking at it as it stands today. All I see is love."

How do you see love in this?

"I see a father who, after working hard all day, manages a few shots with his sons along with the life conversations he had with them under that net. I see brothers who through all of the competition this net instilled, love each other deeply and would move mountains if his brother was in need. I see a mother who not only bandaged the injuries this net brought, but found time shoot a round or two while watching her children grow into strong God-fearing men. I see the love that is still standing."

All too often when we look at the pieces of our life, we get so caught up in the wear and tear that we miss the love that shaped it all.

Yes, we have all been strengthened by the storms of our lives and we carry the scars those days brought. But we are children of a God whose love for us was and is strong enough to keep those pieces from shattering on the ground.

His love is the glue that holds us upright, carries us forward, and keeps us pushing on no matter what this world decides to throw at us.

Take a moment and enjoy the love that is STILL STANDING today and forever!

1 John 3:1
See what great love the Father has lavished on us, that we should be called children of God! And that is what we are! The reason the world does not know us is that it did not know him.

God Doesn't Change

If I would have known what was going to happen, I would have made sure to have before and after photos, but I could not have even imagined what was going to happen. A few nights ago, I went down to help my in-laws prepare for their upcoming party and my job was to power wash the bricks around the garden. Throughout the year friends are encouraged to write their favorite Scripture verse on the bricks in washable marker. Weather and animals have faded the Scriptures and dirtied up the bricks, so my job was to get them ready for the coming event.

There were two Scriptures side by side in this one section that were partially faded, so I readied the power washer, bent low and started to clean the brick. One Scripture came up easily but the other one stayed, and I stopped in my tracks as God spoke…

"I don't change, you do!"

You see, one Scripture was all about God and His sovereignty while the other was all about man and his desire to be more like Christ;

God stayed while man went away. What's really wild is that when I was power washing, I put the wand as close to the brick as I could for the one about God, but my back started to ache from bending over like that, so when I got to the one about man, I stood up straight and the wand was much further away. Logic would dictate that the second Scripture would be the one to stay not the first one; trust me, this power washer will rip your skin wide open if you inadvertently hit your bare foot with it, not that I have ever done that lol.

God's whisper and everything that happened with the bricks had me thinking about my own relationship with my Creator. I can't tell you how many times God has patiently waited for me to return after a prodigal season and then threw a party for me as if I had never run away to begin with. It literally happened one day after He showed me this! I power washed on Wednesday where God spoke to me, and on Thursday I lost my temper over an order not being delivered on time. I changed, God didn't. Even after I so quickly dismissed His teaching, He brought me right back in line today as I mowed the lawn. He remained faithful!

We wax and wane with the coming tide; one minute we are faithfully following God's calling on our lives and the next we are doing the very things He warns us not to do. God stands firm and His love for His creation doesn't change, it deepens, and it beckons.

No matter what season you are trudging through, remember that God is right there with you. His hand is reaching out to you. Take His hand and rest in His love. No matter how many times you stumble, remember that it's His arms that catch you.

He DOES NOT change!

Ephesians 4:11-14
So Christ himself gave the apostles, the prophets, the evangelists, the pastors and teachers, to equip his people for works of service, so that the body of Christ may be built up until we all reach unity in the faith and in the knowledge of the Son of God and become mature, attaining to the whole measure of the fullness of Christ. Then we will no longer be infants, tossed back and forth by the waves, and blown here and there by every wind of teaching and by the cunning and craftiness of people in their deceitful scheming.

Kindness of Strangers

This past week we've had tree trimmers from the county trimming trees along the power lines in both our neighborhood and around our home. The night before they were to start on our property, the foreman came up to me to ask if they could take their vehicles down to the lower field to make trimming and clean-up easier. I was faced with my first choice: let them and risk their heavy vehicles damaging the lower field or force them to carry the trimmings up a steep hill. All I could hear inside my head was, "be nice." I told him it would be no problem for them to go down there, just be careful the closer they got to the lake because the ground is not frozen yet and it's a muddy mess down there. He was grateful and promised to trim a specific tree for us as a thank you.

 The next day the tree trimmers were working hard all day, and when I got home from work one of them came over to see if we wanted the burnable wood they were cutting, or could he have it? Again, I'm faced with a choice: we do in-fact burn wood in the winter and the trees do belong to us, but these guys were working really hard. The voice inside my head repeated, "be nice." So, I said he could absolutely take the wood they were cutting.

The next morning as I'm preparing to leave for work, they are back at it trimming away and I notice that one of their cherry pickers is blocking the driveway, but as I look closer I see that I can get around them, so I finish getting ready. When I go to start my Tahoe, I see that not only is there a cherry picker in the driveway, but there's a work truck as well, and I can't get past the work truck. I start my vehicle to let it warm up and head inside to make my lunch when there is a knock at the door. It's the owner of the work truck who wants to know if I need to leave. I explain that I will be leaving in about 5 minutes and I need the work truck moved, I can get past the cherry picker but not the truck. He explains that because we have been so nice, he's going to move both. When he backs the cherry picker up, he hits our cable line and rips it from the pole.

He's walking toward the house with his head hung down and full of apologies and I'm again faced with a choice: it was an accident, but our cable is now out and it was due to a vehicle he didn't really need to move and I'm now running late for work. In my head that quiet voice says, "be nice just one more time." I explain that it's no problem, we will call the  cable company and get it fixed. He leaves his card just in case the cable company charges for the visit.

My husband calls the cable company and after battling with the automated system they say they will be there that day, then they move it to that night, then they move it to the next morning, and then to the afternoon. My husband is fit to be tied and I have to admit, my blood pressure has risen to a noticeable level. When the worker finally gets there, he asks me to move my vehicle so that he can get a ladder up where the cable connects to the house. Those words keep whispering, "be nice just one more time." I say no problem, explain what happened and then he starts looking at everything. It's going to be more difficult than he first thought, he has to ground it to our house, replace the outside wire, and has to climb a pole to connect it to the cable box, so he's going to be there for quite a while. Again, I hear, "be nice just one more time." I respond that it's no problem. I head inside to finish watching the movie, "Hacksaw Ridge" where Private Dosson repeats over and over, "Okay Lord, help me save just one more."

And it hits me, just one more time. When you're at your wits end, when you can't take it another moment, when you can't do it anymore, do it one more time. God is faithful and will be with you helping you through it, just one more time… and one more time… and one more time. Don't quit, don't lose hope, God's got this!

Galatians 6:9
Let us not become weary doing good, for at the proper time we will reap a harvest if we do not give up."

Memories Come Alive

Yesterday was kind of a crazy day. At work I had a conversation with my pastor where I mentioned that as I began writing a Bible study, I found myself apologizing in the text because I am a visual processor. What that means is that for me to truly comprehend things I have to paint pictures in my mind and that comes out in my writing. People who are verbal processors usually don't care for that type of writing, so I was spending a lot of time apologizing to them for my style. We had a laugh about it, and he reminded me that God created me with this style, I needed to embrace it, and I had nothing to apologize for. I knew this deep down, but it was a good reminder for me.

Then when I got home, I found that I had received two packages from my aunt that contained old family photos. As I plowed through them my brain was filled with childhood memories I had long ago forgotten. There was a memory of my uncle Guy letting me shoot a gun for the first time when I was 5 or 6, he walked me through  what to do, my mom steadied the rifle against my shoulder, and my dad was in the background whispering, "you got this my sweet girl." We were all shocked when I actually hit the target. There was my great grandpa Eckert keeping all of us kids laughing as we waited out a tornado in the root cellar. My brothers and I cutting up at grandma Fenley's house. So many memories, and they were so vivid, I was almost back there again. Why did it take photos for me to see it?

And then God spoke…

"When you study My word, those Scriptures are written on your heart. It's my Holy Spirit living inside you that reminds you of them when you need it most. Much the same way memories from your past are awakened by a photo."

As usual, He was right. When I read Scripture, I paint a picture in my mind of what things might have looked like, I want to feel the emotion hidden within the words; I want to feel Luke's tears hit the page as he pens Paul's final words. Then seemingly out of the blue, those words will come to me in a conversation with a friend, a study group, or even when I'm writing. And when they come to me, I can feel my heart beat just a little faster. It's such an amazing feeling!

For God to love us enough to pen His story on our heart just boggles my mind sometimes. His love knows no bounds, and it all starts with words on a page. Words that build us up and give us hope for something better. Words that paint a picture so beautiful we can't wait to see it face to face.

Don't miss out on that love! READ His word, FEEL His love surround you, BELIEVE the Gospel!

Jeremiah 31:33
"This is the covenant I will make with the people of Israel after that time,"
declares the Lord. "I will put my law in their minds and write it on their hearts.
I will be their God, and they will be my people."

But I Want It!

Over the years of having dogs, I have always enjoyed feeding them some of the scraps while making dinner. Yes, I make sure it's things that are healthy and good for them; that's where this story comes from. You see Tyler seems to think he knows what foods are best for him. The second I told Jake that the scraps were over, he left and went to the living room like every dog I have ever had… except Tyler. I'm cutting a serrano pepper, he has a very sensitive stomach and can't have them; spicy foods make him sick, but he wants it…

And then God spoke…

"Does this remind you of anyone?"

Maybe… yes, it reminds me of me.

"Why do you fight me so hard when I tell you that you won't like what's on the other side of the door you're trying to open?"

Because sometimes my "want to" overrides what I know is right and I start to believe that you're holding out on me.

"Don't you know that I would never try to hurt you or withhold what's best for you?"

I do believe that; I need your help when the "want to" gets too strong.

What do you do when your "want to" is stronger? I know that God only wants what's best for me, but that "want to" is a TOUGH fighter. I think it's what Jesus was talking about when He told His disciples that this evil spirit can only be defeated with PRAYER (Mark 9:29). Prayer is the only thing strong enough for me to fight off the want to spirit within me.

I know that door in-front of you is tempting. It doesn't look like it would hurt you, but God knows that it will, and He's trying to keep you from harm. Tyler expects that serrano to taste like the bell peppers he loves so much, but I know the damage it will do him.

God loves you too much to let you learn the hard way without trying to prevent it. LISTEN TO HIM!

If you're like me, you're going to stumble from time to time, but get back up and try again. He won't leave you, and He will ALWAYS point you the right way.

Proverbs 16:9
In their hearts humans plan their course, but the Lord establishes their steps.

Die to Yourself but Beware of the Remnants

Bob and I have been working on that dreaded bush which is turning out to be a little more difficult than first thought. It will probably take all summer to get it done lol. Last Saturday, we cut a huge grapevine in the hopes that it would make removing some of surrounding bush a little easier. I didn't realize just how much of the bush was actually grapevine. As I was looking at it today, God reminded me that this is what sin looks like in us.

Sin doesn't just enter one part of our life; it has a tendency to weave its deadly poison all around and in every crevice of our lives. So,  when we "die to ourselves" as the Apostle Paul tells us, we have to always beware of the remnants and make sure that we remove it all. Remnants can be just as detrimental as the sin itself, sometimes it prevents us from doing to things God has called us to because fear is still there. What if I fail? What if I'm not good enough? What if they pick someone else because of my past? What if… and the poison builds again…

Faith is the only answer to sweeping out the "remnants" and letting us learn to trust that God really does HAVE THIS! It helps us to turn the "what if I fail?" to, "what if I succeed?" God is not only our comforter, but He is our defender and our greatest champion. His love knows no

bounds, and He knows the crevices where our past sin hides.

Trust Him when He says it's time to sweep out the remnants and FILL it with HIS truths for you!

Matthew 12:43-45

"When an impure spirit comes out of a person, it goes through arid places seeking rest and does not find it. Then it says, 'I will return to the house I left.' When it arrives, it finds the house unoccupied, swept clean and put in order. Then it goes and takes with it seven other spirits more wicked than itself, and they go in and live there. And the final condition of that person is worse than the first. That is how it will be with this wicked generation."

Crimson Red to Snow White

For the sake of our stomachs I chose not to take pictures. Mondays are normally the day that I write the Bible study I have been working on, but I have been interrupted so much today that I set it aside until later this evening. From the pest control guy, to phone calls, to dogs in trouble it has been chaos in the house today. It makes not only writing complicated, but just about everything I need to get done today. I don't function well when I'm distracted, and I know that.

Because Bob is working from home, he's eating lunch at home, and to save money, I make the salads that he prefers to have for lunch for him. It's cheaper to make it yourself rather than buying the ready made ones, so since I was already distracted I decided to go ahead and make it in the hopes that the chaos would calm down by the time I was done. He likes turnips, carrots, and radishes mixed in with the different lettuces, so to make it look like the ones in the store I use a mandolin to cut them vs. cutting them with a knife. You can already tell where this is going can't you? Yes, I was distracted while using the mandolin, and I proceeded to slice off the tip of my middle finger. As with head wounds, finger wounds can bleed profusely and this one was no different. As I'm trying get it to stop bleeding long enough to get a band aid on it, I'm making a mess and blood is dripping everywhere.

And God spoke... can we stop here for just a second... I'm in pain, my finger is throbbing, blood is everywhere, and God speaks! My first thought was you couldn't speak before that mandolin bit my finger? But I digress...

"Do you see Me working in the chaos?"

Most of the time, but I do miss it occasionally

"Is that your doing or mine?"

It's mine.

"Then why do you blame Me?"

Because I expect you to point it out before I miss it.

"And what do you tell people who place that expectation on you?"

Do you know how frustrating it is to have your own words used against you?

I had no argument to God's question because I know that I routinely tell people who place me in that position, that I'm honored you think that much of me, but I will never be able to meet that expectation. Sometimes I place expectations on God that go against His promise of free will. How about you?

In the below passage Isaiah is explaining to both Judah and Jerusalem that their distracted free will has blinded them to the workings of God and they are about to go through some pain, but in the end, their crimson red sin will be washed clean by God and they will be white as snow. Their pain will be a growing process and will serve to draw them closer to the lover of their souls.

May we all learn to see God working in the midst of our chaos and distraction before we are injured. But in those moments when we don't, may we be open to the teachings He has designed specifically for us.

Isaiah 1:18
"Come now, let us settle the matter," says the Lord. "Though your sins are like scarlet, they shall be as white as snow; though they are red as crimson, they shall be like wool.

Focus

I HATE being sick! I am the worst patient on the planet. I sleep to the point that all of my joints ache and I struggle moving around the house. I had all of these plans for my staycation, and they all went out the window with my sixteen to eighteen hour a day sleep necessity!

Then God got ahold of me…

"Do you believe in Me?" He asked my response was yes, and then He asked, "do you trust me?" Again, my answer is yes, and totally confused at why I am being asked this. His response… if you truly trust Me and believe in Me, why do I have to let you get sick to get you to slow down and focus SOLELY on Me?

The last few weeks I have been running from direction to another with barely enough time to breathe let alone focus solely on God. Don't get me wrong, He was there, but not COMPLETELY, and He should have been. I was so busy at work that usually, by the time I got home I was crashing on the couch and vegging out on T.V. Not only did I not take the time to thank God for being my rock all day, but I also didn't stop throughout the day to say WOW, I can't believe You just did that! Time and time again He showed up in big ways, and I missed it… until I was sick…

Take time to recognize not only who you are, but Whose you are. God moves in each of us in so many incredible ways, and He shows us when we FOCUS on Him. He is our Rock and Redeemer. BELIEVE it!

1 Peter 1:8
Though you have not seen him, you love him; and even though you do not see him now, you believe in him and are filled with an inexpressible and glorious joy.

Trust in the Transition

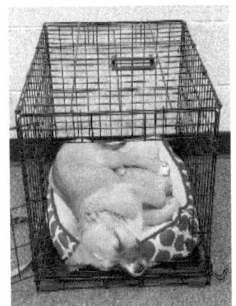

When we first brought Jake into our home, he wasn't super thrilled with the cage we had for him. He was confined to a small space while Tyler was allowed to roam free. As a result, Jake was forced to be alone in the living room for short periods of time. Before coming home with us he always had at least one of his siblings with him and he was never alone. Needless to say, Jake was not happy with this transition. He didn't understand what Bob and I knew that the cage will eventually become his safe place to sleep and to get away from the chaos that sometimes surrounds our home.

Knowing I would be alone at work for the first hour and that Jake wouldn't interfere with anyone I let him run around the office and just left the cage door open. After a while, I didn't hear the pitter patter of his feet chasing ball around the room, so I looked down to see him sound asleep IN his cage. Even when other people came in, I left the cage door open and Jake went in and out, playing for a little while and then napping for a little while. With a smile on my face I whispered, "I'm so glad your part of my life, and I love that you are beginning to trust me with this cage."

And then God spoke...

"That's a lot like our relationship, isn't it?"

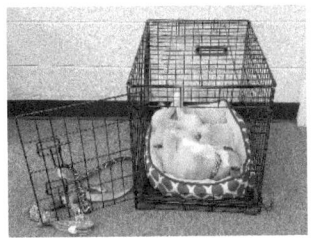

What do you mean?

"I give you simple things to start with, asking you to trust Me in the transitions of our relationship. You don't like it at first, you even fight me from time to time, but then all of the sudden you see that what I've created is a safe place for you amidst the chaos of this world. I love it when you see the safety of our relationship, and I love you!"

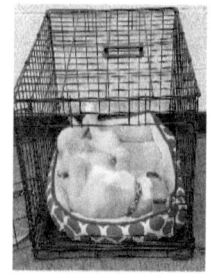

What are you wrestling with God over? Can you trust Him with the outcome?

Sometimes what God asks of us seems impossible, it's just not who we are or what we want to do. Realizing that it's just temporary is tough, I know I routinely struggle with it. But just like Jake, I'm learning that the on other side of the struggle is the safety and security of someone who loves me like no other.

TRUST HIM IN THE TRANSITION.
The love on the other side of the struggle is worth every battle!

Romans 15:13
May the God of hope fill you with all joy and peace as you trust in him, so that you may overflow with hope by the power of the Holy Spirit.

Set Apart

There's this deer that we've seen every morning and evening for the last few years. We discovered that she's been living in the swamp by my mother-in-law's house. She comes  over to our house simply because she loves our vegetation, specifically the wild raspberry that's everywhere on our property. As I was taking some photos of her yesterday, I couldn't help but question why she's living around here. The swamp is damp and cold, and it's surrounded by houses and water; not to mention, she's by herself and not with a herd. When she has babies, they stay with her for a season and then leave and she's alone again.

And then God spoke…

"She's doing what I ask you and all those who believe in me to do; she set herself apart. She has everything she needs right where she's at and she lacks for nothing."

Don't misunderstand, God doesn't call us to be alone and lonely. He does however call us to set ourselves apart from the world and trust in Him to provide for our every need. That doe has had two  sets of twins in the time that she's been here, so she's far from lonely. But in setting herself apart, she truly lacks for nothing. There's a herd of deer less than a mile from that swamp, and I have no doubt she would be welcomed in, and yet she stays where she at. That herd is routinely thinned out by passing cars and fall hunters, but because she has remained in the swamp, she's safe and secure from those dangers as well as others.

If only we could learn from her!

I know from experience that when I fully lean in to God and set myself apart in all ways, I have not missed out on anything, but then something comes along, catches my attention and I allow myself to be swayed back into worldly thinking. What about you?

There's a verse in chapter 2 of the Song of Songs where Solomon warns us to be aware of the distractions that lead to destruction. And just like this devotional, it deals with wildlife.

Song of Songs 2:15
"Catch for us the foxes, the little foxes that ruin the vineyards, our vineyards that are in bloom."

Think about it for just a second…

The fox means well, and they are actually doing a good thing. They  are hunting the animals that make their dens around the vines weakening the vineyard, but as the fox digs for their prey they inadvertently destroy the roots. When was the last time a friend, co-worker, family member, television show, news report, or social media post distracted you from something you knew you were supposed to do?

Beware of the fox my friends. Set yourself apart like the deer.

Lean into God and let Him provide for your every need!

Proverbs 3:5-6
Trust in the Lord with all your heart and lean not on your own understanding; in all your ways submit to him, and he will make your paths straight.

Got Faith?

There's a lot of faith out there: radical faith, bold faith, crazy faith, deep faith, easy faith, reckless faith, unbelievable faith, and the list goes on and on. From Abraham to Paul to you and I, we all have to  have some type of faith to thrive in this world, but what does that really mean? In the job that I am so blessed to do, I see the extremes on each side, people faithful in prayer have those prayers miraculously answered and yet people faithful in prayer walk away feeling virtually empty as their prayers are devastatingly not answered. This quagmire has people everywhere questioning the very existence of God, and pastors are forced to try answering questions that have no answer other than faith doesn't guarantee answers this side of heaven. This has been my conversation with Jesus this week.

When our faith and our desire to control run headfirst into each other, the fireworks begin. I know many of you, like me, have said the prayer, "God if you... then I will..." or maybe "God I need... in order to serve you better" or even, "God, if only you would... it would be so much easier to..." I am finding that when my faith in God is tested, I run quickly to controlling whatever is causing the  test. God's answer is simple, yet so stinken complicated, "trust in Me alone, let go of control, and have faith that My will is going to be done even when the answer is not what you wanted."

Author James Frey writes, "loss of control is always the source of fear, it is also, however, always the source of change." God's desire is an unhindered relationship with us, and He knows that control gets in the way of that. What's it going to take for us to figure that one out? I strive for that unhindered relationship daily, and I fight hard against my desire to control things around me. A few days ago,

I asked the question, "where does your trust in God stop?" My trust has a tendency to stop when I realize I have no control over something, and that is the thorn I battle. What about you? Will I live in fear, or embrace the changes loss of control brings? Like with you, the choice is mine.

The God of the universe wants a relationship with you and me. He  wants us to choose Him. Life will be hard at times, our prayers will be answered, but not always the way we want, but most of all, God will love us with a love that knows no bounds. Is that enough? Can we have faith enough to relinquish control? If it's the last thing I do, I intend to learn how! Join me.

Got faith?

Hebrews 11:1
Now faith is confidence in what we hope for and assurance about what we do not see.

I Want to but it's Hard

The other day my husband pointed out these icicles. On one side of the prayer room, there are a bunch of them, and they are as straight as can be, but on the other side there's only one, and it's crooked.  The straight ones don't have any obstacles, they are protected from the wind, the water came over the top of the gutter and froze on the way down making them as straight as they are meant to be. The one all by itself is on the other side where there's wind from multiple angles, and the water trickled out of a hole in the back of the gutter; angle, wind, and gravity didn't allow it to flow straight. It want's to, but it's hard.

I was pondering the difficulties of the one when God spoke…

"Why do you continually choose to compare?"

When I want to move forward and advance, I need something to gauge where I'm at vs. where I'm going.

"But comparison is the wrong tool."

What do you mean?

"You're pitting their highlight reel against your b-roll."

… hmm

"Those people you're comparing yourself to, were you there when they fought through the sleepless nights of doubt? What about when they battled their own demons and came away beaten and bloody, were you there for that? Were you holding them up when their knees buckled under the weight of their own perceived shortcomings?"

… no

"I was there EVERY time."

… oof

"Each of my children has a perfect path designed solely for them. You move forward in MY strength, not your own."

God's path for each of us is filled with ups and downs, twists and turns, good and bad, but we are NEVER alone. We may wind up with bumps and bruises, our path may have us bending beyond what we think is possible, but it's His arms that carry us through. If you're like me, you want to stand straight and tall, but it's hard, especially when we use comparison as a tool. Our b-roll will never stand up to their highlight reel. STOP

God's design for you is PERFECT!

Hebrews 13:20-21
Now may the God of peace, who through the blood of the eternal covenant brought back from the dead our Lord Jesus, that great Shepherd of the sheep, equip you with everything good for doing his will, and may he work in us what is pleasing to him, through Jesus Christ, to whom be glory for ever and ever. Amen.

An Eagle When She Flies

Just a few hours ago my mother-in-law called down to say that
 there was a bald eagle in the willow tree down by
the lake. We used binoculars first, then I went in
and got my camera. Because it's gray and hazy out
the photos don't quite do what we witnessed
justice, but it was still a sight to see. As I slowly
walked down to see how close I could get, a second
eagle flew in followed by a third.

As they began to fly off, a song entered my head, it's still stuck
there now. Most of you know I'm a country music fan, and the
song that ran through my brain was Dolly Parton's "Eagle When
She Flies." While listening to the song in my head, images of my
grandmother raced in. This is her
birthday month, and if she were still
here, she would be turning 100 at the
end of the month. What I wouldn't
give to feel one of her hugs again. The
lyrics fit her so well, it's hard to hold
back the tears. "Gentle as the sweet magnolia. Strong as steel, her
faith and pride. She's an everlasting shoulder. She's the leaning post
of life. She hurts deep and when she weeps. She's just as fragile as a
child. And she's a sparrow when she's broken. But she's an eagle
when she flies."

 She was the first one to use the words
Jesus Christ as something more than a
cuss word to me. She planted the seed that
would later grow into the woman capable
of writing this. My faith in God is a result
of her steel embraced magnolia life and
the time I was blessed to share with her.

This afternoon was the most beautiful kiss from God that I have
had in a long time. While I may shed the tears of missing her, I
remember her with a joy that words will never truly justify.

The person who first introduced you to your Savior. The youth leader who walked with you through your storm. The pastor who reached out when you didn't have the strength to. Remember them with a smile, reach out to them if you can, be grateful for all of those God has put on your path. Praise Him for bringing them into your life.

God places people in our path to help us along our journey. They draw us to a deeper more personal relationship with Him. That's something to be marveled and celebrated. He loves us ALL so much that He will move heaven and earth to reach us.

Today I celebrate. How about you?

Psalm 103:1-5
Praise the Lord, my soul; all my inmost being, praise his holy name. Praise the Lord, my soul, and forget not all his benefits—who forgives all your sins and heals all your diseases, who redeems your life from the pit and crowns you with love and compassion, who satisfies your desires with good things so that your youth is renewed like the eagle's.

Strength in Weakness

We had some new neighbors move in recently, and they love to decorate their yard. It's always fun to drive or walk by just to see what new thing they have done. About mid-September they put up their fall decorations and started the Halloween ones. They also put up this sign.

I was so curious about it, and what it meant that I looked it up on the internet to see what I could find out. When I read what it was

 about, I was even more confused because it didn't match the sign. Bob and I had even talked about a few times, and I couldn't figure it out. I have been driving and walking past this sign for over six weeks now. I discovered today that I have been reading it wrong all this time. My dyslexia kicked in without me knowing it, so what I saw was, "Free the Padre Pio. Prayer TRIALS." But as you can clearly see, it actually says, "Free, the Padre Pio prayer TRAILS." This makes total sense with what I read on-line.

When I discovered that my dyslexia reared its ugly imperfect head, I was so mad at myself. All I could think was what an idiot I was for not catching that. I even missed the flip when I looked it up on-line. I must have looked like a fool to my husband who graciously said nothing.

I was in full beat myself up mode when God spoke...

"Why are you so angry?"

I can't believe I let this stupid glitch in me trip me up for so long.

"Why didn't you ask me about it?"

It was just a sign.

"Those 'little' things are what I cherish most about our relationship. It's in those moments that my strength shines the brightest in you. My strength in your weakness… that's the perfect combination!"

It's so easy for me to get caught up in "I can do it in my own strength" mentality. It takes effort on my part to realize that there is not a single thing big or small in my life that doesn't matter to God. He wants to be a part of EVERYTHING! And I should let Him, because things move so much smoother when He's there. Don't get me wrong, I still go through pain and struggles, but knowing that He's got me makes it so much more peaceful to walk through the storm.

What about you? What's that mentality God is asking you to lay at His feet? God wants to be a part of it all… LET HIM IN!

2 Corinthians 12:9-10
But he said to me, "My grace is sufficient for you, for my power is made perfect in weakness." Therefore I will boast all the more gladly about my weaknesses, so that Christ's power may rest on me. That is why, for Christ's sake, I delight in weaknesses, in insults, in hardships, in persecutions, in difficulties. For when I am weak, then I am strong.

Rivalry or Compassion

Sandhill cranes suffer from what is commonly called Cain and Abel syndrome. In this, adults hatch two eggs, and then feed the one that  fights the hardest for the food. The siblings peck at each other continually and eventually when one gets the upper hand and is stronger, it will kill its weaker sibling. My in-laws have a pair at their house where this is happening. It is very rare, but every now and then, one pair will actually work together moving back and forth between the parents to get food and both survive. This seems to be the pair we have at our house. Both are growing strong and will likely survive to adulthood.

I was marveling at this when God spoke…

"What is it that causes anger when you speak to My children?"

It can be what they say or what they stand for. I try not to, but sometimes I struggle controlling my attitude when someone says or does something that I wholeheartedly disagree with.

"But that's where I call you to have compassion, not rivalry."

 I get that, but sometimes it's hard. Look at the world today, we are just an angry bunch of people!

"What is more important, being My child, or being right?"

That question still cuts to the core!

I know it's more important to be God's child, and when that gets in the way of me being right I have to force my mouth shut. I have to walk away from my computer or phone and not hit send on a message or post that I really want to.

There are a multitude of reasons to be angry today, our world is falling apart, and we are all feeling forced to take sides. Taking sides doesn't mean we have to become "Cain and Abel," we have an opportunity to show the light of Christ to a dying world. We all have differing opinions on the current state of things and that's okay. What matters is that we work together as children of Christ and remain obedient to God's call on each of our lives.

If you're like me, you have had to hit the delete button more than once in a day, and your tongue is pretty tender from all the biting you have had to do to it.

It's worth it!

John 13:34-35
 "A new command I give you: Love one another. As I have loved you, so you must love one another. By this everyone will know that you are my disciples, if you love one another."

It's Not Complicated

My husband and I have this game where one of us will ask our dog(s) a question, and the other will answer as if we were the dog. This morning as we were finishing breakfast, we noticed that Jake was sleeping with his head on the arm of the loveseat, and as a result of gravity his tongue was sticking out. I made the remark, "that can't be a comfortable position," to which my husband replied for Jake, "play hard sleep hard mama!" It was a comical but also very true statement. As Jake is getting bigger, his appetite for play has increased as well. Both Tyler and I have had to wave the white flag of surrender multiple times. When play time is finally over, he crashes equally as hard, and often in very strange positions. As a mama, it's my job to photograph these memories, and as you can see, I thoroughly enjoy this task. As I snapped the photo, my husband's words rang through my head, and…

God spoke…

"Do you see how simple that puppy's life is?"

What do you mean?

"He plays hard and sleeps hard. He looks to you for his nourishment when he wakes and protection when he sleeps. That's the life I want for you and for all of my children!"

It's NOT that simple! Life throws me more curveballs than it throws Jake.

But it IS that simple. The other night when Jake got the twig stuck in his mouth, he tried to get it out himself as he was walking toward you. When he couldn't get it out, he sat down at your feet and

waited for you to fix it. If you would walk toward me as you try to fix your situations, and then sit at my feet when you can't and wait for me, those curveballs wouldn't be so difficult and there wouldn't be as many. It's not complicated baby, just move toward me and then be still."

As usual, He's right!

I know, I know, easier said than done… I'm right there with you, but how simple would our lives actually be if we moved toward Him and then waited at His feet. It really isn't as complicated as we make it seem.

Life throws lots of curveballs, but Jesus is always the fix! No matter how big of a mess I make, He ALWAYS knows just how to fix it and make it better. We still get to play hard, work hard, and make dumb mistakes, but there's something about the knowledge that God has me in the shelter of His wing that will allow me to sleep hard in the security of knowing He's GOT this!

And… HE'S GOT YOU!

Luke 10:39
She (Martha) had a sister called Mary, who sat at the Lord's feet listening to what he said.

Hope

Have you ever had a Scripture leap off the page and take you on a journey in your mind that you never saw coming?

I was doing some studying when I looked at my verse for the day, and even though I have read Romans multiple times, this verse has never caught my attention, until today. *"For everything that was written in the past was written to teach us, so that through the endurance taught in the Scriptures and the encouragement they provide we might have hope."* – Romans 15:4

Out of the blue I had visions of several stories regarding patience and ability to walk through tough situations found throughout the Old Testament. That vivid imagery moved from Noah spending over forty years building an ark all while being called a fool before the first drop of rain fell, to Malachi wrestling to lead a group of incredibly unhappy Israelites back home following seventy years in exile in Babylon. The endurance they all had to show is mind boggling to me. But what's even more unbelievable to me is that they went through all of that to give hope to you and me.

It was written down and taught to believers over the centuries so that when we face rough times and are hurting so much that we can't see around the corner of our circumstances we can rest assured that God is with us and for us. He will make a way where it doesn't seem fathomable.

While it's not written in the Bible, I can't help but see as Job sat down with his grandchildren to tell his story and he made sure to say, "now you make sure you write this down so that …*insert your name here…* will know that our Creator Redeemer loves them more than they could ever dream of.

He is real. He is right here, arms stretched wide whispering, *"Come to me, all you who are weary and burdened, and I will give you rest."* – Matthew 11:28

True Identity

Do you ever have those moments when you really want to say something to someone, but you're not sure whether or not you should? You don't know if what you say would be beneficial or hurtful? Lately I have found myself wrestling with different Biblical theologies, there are some that my studies have shown to be highly accurate and some not so much. All of them can and do lead people to Christ, but if a person takes too hard of a stance, they can also lead people astray. I try to be very well rounded and listen to all of them, but if I'm honest, there are a few that I really have a hard time with. When I hear friends or family talk about how great one of those theologies are, I want to scream at the top of my lungs for them to get as far away from that belief as possible.

I was running all of this through my head earlier when I noticed that our home is being invaded by the stink bug. Much like the theologies, some stink bugs are highly beneficial and others not so much. The good ones feed on caterpillars, moths, aphids, and other harmful beetles; they protect the local plant life. The bad ones however, feed on the plant life and are known to destroy entire crops. Identifying the difference between the good and the bad ones is very difficult; good ones have small spines on their shoulders and the bad ones don't. Trying to see these spines with my older eyes is not so easy anymore.

All of this stuff was beating up my brain when God spoke...

"Why do you wrestle so hard with things that only I control?"

I don't want my friends and family to be hurt.

"If you trust Me with them, the pain they feel will be growing pains designed to make them stronger."

But what if they are led away from You?

"Then it's up to Me to woo them back. Everyone has free will to choose, not just you. You worry about OUR relationship, not theirs."

Sometimes that's a hard pill to swallow! I hate seeing people make bad choices, but then I have to remember the life lessons God taught me in my wrong choice moments. As rough as those times were, I believe I'm a better person for it.

 Whether you're a new covenant saint, a dispensationalist, covenant theologian, prosperity gospel believer, follower of the hyper grace philosophy, or any of the others in-between may God meet you there and show you each and every truth the Gospel has for you. May your relationship with Christ be the most fulfilling thing you ever walk through.

My prayer for us all is that God blesses each and every one of us beyond anything we could possibly ask or imagine!

Matthew 6:33
But seek first his kingdom and his righteousness, and all these things will be given to you as well.

Voices

This morning as I was downloading some photos I had taken last week, I came across the ones of this little bird singing. Since they are not great shots, I was debating deleting them when God whispered, "if they keep quiet, the stones will cry out."

 You see, I love catching the birds in poses as they are shouting their good mornings, or good nights, or where's my buddies, and this little guy is by far the loudest of them all. The crows and redwing blackbirds have nothing on him when he opens up those vocal chords. I don't know what he is, but I realized he is the one that wakes me up every morning; he's the one I hear above the sparrows and the mourning doves, and he is a fraction of their size...

"If they keep quiet the stones will cry out."

We all have a voice deserving and needing to be heard above the noise of this world. Too often we lie to ourselves and say, "no one is listening," or "no one cares what I have to say," or "I should wait until things calm down." I could go on with the lies we believe, but I don't feel like that's the point God was making to me this morning. I believe He's telling us to speak.

When we see a miracle of God, speak it out loud for everyone to hear.

When we see an atrocity, raise our voices above the noise.

When we are given wisdom, share it with all who will listen.

When we are lonely and hurting, reach out, even if all we have is a whisper.

Let's stop hiding our voices behind chaos this world brings. We've gotten to this place because we were too afraid, too unsure, too timid, too whatever. Our "too's" are over…

IF WE KEEP QUIET THE STONES WILL CRY OUT!

It's time to stand up and be heard!

Luke 19:37-40
When he came near the place where the road goes down the Mount of Olives, the whole crowd of disciples began joyfully to praise God in loud voices for all the miracles they had seen: "Blessed is the king who comes in the name of the Lord!" "Peace in heaven and glory in the highest!" Some of the Pharisees in the crowd said to Jesus, "Teacher, rebuke your disciples!" "I tell you," he replied, "if they keep quiet, the stones will cry out."

Good Vs. Important

I've been a little under the weather the last week or so, most likely an allergy induced sinus infection, but it has me a little sensitive to the elements. As I was preparing to make breakfast, my mother-in-law called to say that the eagle had returned and was in the willow tree down by the lake. I grabbed my camera, put on my shoes and headed out without a jacket. As I slowly walked down to see how close I could get the cold set in on my shoulders; I wasn't going to be able to stay out long.

I was happily snapping photos when our neighbor let his dog out and the barking began because I was too close to his fence. Curious at what was happening the neighbor slowly  walked over to not only quiet his dog, but to say hi to me. As we conversed the eagle took off, and I missed my favorite shot when they first take flight. My focus was on my neighbor, and not the eagle. As we said our goodbyes, I headed back to the house, uncomfortably cold and feeling a little dejected over missing the shot.

And then God spoke...

"Why does following My call bother you so much?"

It's not that it bothers me, I just really cold now, and I didn't get the good shot. I don't see the eagles very often, so I just wanted to try for that shot.

"What was more important?"

Can I just say I really don't like it when He pulls the "more important" card! But alas, He was right, taking time to talk with a friend and show the love of Christ is much more important than any photo opportunity. What's really funny is that I just talked about this during my churches Flashcard Friday message. Sometimes I get so caught up in doing good things that if I'm not careful I can miss out on the important things. How about you?

What's more important, winterizing your boat or taking a walk with your spouse? A business meeting on your day off or your child's soccer game?

Don't miss out on important because you're too busy doing good! Trust the nudge of the Holy Spirit in your life.

1 Peter 2:4-5
As you come to him, the living Stone—rejected by humans but chosen by God and precious to him—you also, like living stones, are being built into a spiritual house to be a holy priesthood, offering spiritual sacrifices acceptable to God through Jesus Christ.

Changes

NO SHOOTING THE MESSENGER!!!! While I was walking around the yard this afternoon, I noticed that Fall is just around the corner and some of our trees are already starting to show the coming change in seasons. Not all of the leaves in these trees have changed, they seem to each be on their own schedule, and some are still green while others are varying shades of yellow and red. It had me thinking about us as Christ followers and how we don't all change at the same time...

Each of us follows a pattern that God has designed for us, our choices and God's nudges move us from point to point, but at different speeds from each other. Too often we see people get frustrated with others around them and their lack of growth, or we question the depth of their growth because of the speed with which they are moving. And guess what? It's not our job to determine

someone else's speed; God through the Holy Spirit determines how much and how quickly we change. It's really easy to see someone else's flaws and where they need to move to next, but I know that when I am faced with this, it's usually because I have a flaw or two that I am trying to remain in denial about. Billy Graham said it best when he said, "It's the HOLY SPIRIT'S job to convict, GOD'S Job to judge, and it's MY job to love.

When we focus on our own relationship with God and learn to love others where they are, I believe that He smiles the widest smile a Father can possibly smile. That's all I want to see!!! How about you?

Psalm 15
A psalm of David.
LORD, *who may dwell in your sacred tent? Who may live on your holy mountain? The one whose walk is blameless, who does what is righteous, who speaks the truth from their heart; whose tongue utters no slander, who does no wrong to a neighbor, and casts no slur on others; who despises a vile person but honors those who fear the* LORD*; who keeps an oath even when it hurts, and does not change their mind; who lends money to the poor without interest; who does not accept a bribe against the innocent. Whoever does these things will never be shaken.*

Missing Signs

There is no photography for this devotional, and that is precisely why this one is being written. As I was cooking breakfast this morning, I looked out toward the lake and watched this beautiful shiny black squirrel climb up our ash tree and sit out at the very edge of a limb. I thought it was pretty cool, then I went back to cooking breakfast and didn't give it another thought.

As I was preparing to get some computer work done a few hours later, God spoke...

"Why do you miss the things I put right in front of you?"

I don't understand, what did I miss?

"You ask Me to guide you in writing these devotionals, and yet when I give you a photo op, you say, 'that's cool' and move on with your day."

As I walked back to the window and found the squirrel long gone, all I heard was, "That moment is gone, it's time to move forward, but open your eyes baby."

1 Peter 5:8
Be alert and of sober mind. Your enemy the devil prowls around like a roaring lion looking for someone to devour.

Usually when this is read, we say it as if it were one sentence, but if you take a closer look you will see that it's not; it is actually two sentences. *"Be alert and of sober mind."* Is both attached to the next sentence because of the verse numbering, but also separate due to the period. We absolutely need to be alert to the schemes of the devil, but God has been challenging me to be alert to the signs and wonders that He places in my path. God can be found in so many simple things if we would just take the time to notice.

The squirrel climbed the ash tree to see what dangers there are in his area; he was also looking for potential gains of food and shelter.

This little creature created by God was exemplifying those words found in the Scripture and teaching me in the process.

God's wonders and signs surround us each and every day, but we have to take the blinders off in order to see them. Be ALERT for the prowling devil, but also, be ALERT to the miracles God has placed in our path to help us in battling the devil.

My signs come from what I see in nature. Where do your signs come from? Do you see them? Do you heed them?

Daniel 4:3
How great are his signs, how mighty his wonders! His kingdom is an eternal kingdom; his dominion endures from generation to generation.

Our Plans... And God...

When my husband's grandfather owned this property, he used to place things that needed repairing on the fence line next to the barn where he did all of that kind of work. He had a system and an order to all of it. As health issues began to take their toll, instead of mowing over the unwanted swamp bushes he started mowing next to them, slowly they crept deeper into the yard covering up the projects he was no longer able to take care of. Fast forward twenty-five years and my husband is now slowly removing all of the bushes and reclaiming the fence line while exposing all of the deteriorating projects. Seeing these bring back fond memories of his grandfather and all of the things they used to do together when my husband was a child.

I was admiring the hard work my husband has been doing when God spoke...

"Why do you think so little of yourself?"

Where did that come from?

"Each time you say you don't think that's where you belong or that you should be doing that, I put you in a position to accomplish that very thing just to show you that you can do anything... with Me."

When I overstep it gets me in a lot of trouble; I guess it's made me timid.

"I held your husband's grandfather through his life, and he did amazing things with and for Me. I carry your husband through his ups and downs, and he is doing incredible things with and for Me. Why do you doubt I would do that for you?"

Oh, how I wish I had a logical answer to that question. God has done so many wonderful things in my life and yet I routinely think I've gone as far I can, and I make plans around my limitations. And then God chuckles and pushes me further than I thought possible. It's not always comfortable, but He is faithful to stay with me through it all.

Where are you limiting yourself? Is God calling you deeper?

Let Go, Let God!

Mark 10:27
Jesus looked at them and said, "With man this is impossible, but not with God; all things are possible with God."

Unseen

My husband and I live in a home that
was built in 1942 on a lake. I love this
house, but there are gaps and drafts
and little things that we are fixing one
by one when we can. It's not unusual
to find copious amounts of bugs, and
spiders, it's just part of lake life in an

old house. We have even stumbled across a baby snake in the
basement. Last year, we decided to try a pest control company that
uses 99% essential oils, the 1% is solely to kill silver beetles. We
were skeptical to say the least because we have always had bugs and
spiders in the house.

We have been pleasantly surprised that since June we have only had
to deal with gyspy moths in the house, and apparently there is no
cure for those. Since June I have not had to kill a single spider, fly,
silver beetle, or ear wig. So, I was completely baffled when I
stumbled across this massive spider web while cleaning the living
room. How could we miss a spider capable of creating such a
masterpiece?

And then God spoke…

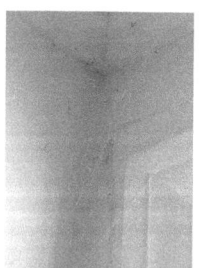
"Can you have a spider web without a spider?"

No.

"What else are you not seeing?"

I don't know.

"You see My Son in the things of this world, but do you see the evil
that fights hard for control over you?"

Not always.

"If the devil gets a foothold, he will take your focus off of where it belongs, on Me."

As much as we love seeing the amazing things God puts in our path, we need to be aware of the traps the devil has designed to trip us up. He doesn't deserve our focus, but we have to admit that he exists and desires to draw us away from our Divine Protector.

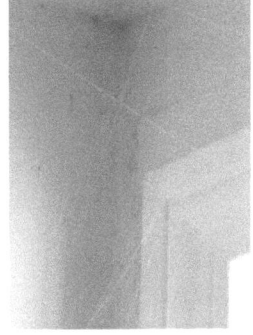

Spiritual warfare is taking place all around us, and we are the prize. It's subtle, sneaky, and we don't always see what's happening. Much like that mystery spider in the house, things happen in our lives, and doubt creeps in, and before we know it, we are caught in a web designed to take our focus off the plan that God has for us. When we have that nagging, "see, you're not good enough…" or, "you messed up again, why do you keep trying…" or even the patented, "did God really say…" we can't give in. Jesus is our foundation. He's the Rock that will carry us through, but only if we pay attention and hold tightly to the promise that He will ruin the schemes of the devil.

Our ultimate Defender loves us and will help prevent us from drifting away. BELIEVE THAT! TRUST THAT!

Isaiah 42:23
Which of you will listen to this or pay close attention in time to come?

Walk a Mile

Because the forecast was going to be too hot today, I decided to mow the lawn last night. While I was mowing my husband and brother-in-law were burning brush created when the county trimmed trees on our property that were too close to the power lines. It was a beautiful night, temperature, humidity, and wind were just right, and we are all working while others play on the lake. Kayakers and boaters looked like they were having a great time and instantly I was a little frustrated.

It seems like when you live on a lake, work is never done. Fence-lines need cleaned up, brush needs burned, weeds need to be pulled, lawn needs mowed, and the list goes on and on. Sometimes it's irritating to watch others having fun while you're working so hard, and you just want to call out their laziness.

And then God spoke…

If you're like me, you might be thinking that God pulled out the story of Mary and Martha. And you would be wrong, He went to Matthew 7. He nudged my eye toward the young man on the kayak and asked a simple question, "What kind of a day do you think he had today?"

I don't know.

"That's right you don't, but I do. He's right where he needs to be, and so are you. You are both in a position to deepen your relationship with me."

I was totally judging that young man; I was feeling like I deserved to be there, and he didn't. To top it all off, I wanted to be where he was at, but my motive was purely selfish. It was based on pleasure not on developing the relationship with my Creator. Mowing the lawn is where I feel closest to God, and I wanted to trade that for some temporary fun on the water.

Sometimes we play, sometimes we work, but God has to be in the center of it, or it's meaningless. I know that in my head, but last night my heart needed to see it. The reality is that I actually love mowing the lawn and I cherish the teachings God walks me through. I do love to kayak, but I love spending time with God more;  my heart knows and believes that now.

Where do you hear from God the loudest? Strive to be there above anywhere else; you won't be disappointed if you do!

Matthew 7:1-2
Do not judge, or you too will be judged. For in the same way you judge others, you will be judged, and with the measure you use, it will be measured to you.

What is Underneath?

Snowmageddon 2022 found me with an unexpected day off from my church administrative duties, and Jake decided he wanted to celebrate that with an early afternoon play date in the snow. I brought my camera to take pictures of Jake and Tyler but found myself enamored with the snow. From the complex design of the snowflake to the way they weave themselves on top of the different tree limbs I was completely fascinated. I noticed the tree limbs underneath, but I was more interested in what was on top.

Then God spoke…

"Why do my children refuse to dig deep into my word and see all that I have underneath?"

Digging deep is hard. Before you know it, you are so far down the rabbit hole and finding your way out is tough!

"But don't you do that every time something goes wrong? You tear yourself down trying to get to what's underneath, and you wind up in a rabbit hole of self-hate and doubt that you struggle getting out of until you turn to Me."

Can we talk for a minute? Have you ever had God leave you speechless? I mean so speechless that it takes a tractor to pick your jaw up off the floor? That's me right now!

It's so easy to dig into my back story and find flaws, so why is it so hard to dig into God's word and find His redemption in-between the pages? I know myself, I know the good and the bad, so it is super easy to beat myself up and only take a look at the bad. If I only look at Scripture by itself, God looks like a stern browed disciplinarian just waiting for me to screw up, that's easy. If I look deep, if I look at His word in context and how He meets all of us where we are in culture, then I have to admit that He is looking to redeem me with the grace of a loving and compassionate Father. That's a hard pill to swallow!

But it is SO WORTH IT!

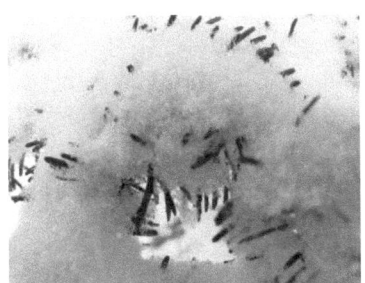 From Genesis 1:1 all the way to Revelation 22:21, if you are willing to dig in and discover what is underneath, you WILL find a Creator Redeemer who longs to restore every moment you have given to the locusts of your past.

Looking at the limbs underneath the snow, I discovered new buds preparing for spring, and bark tightening around the limb to keep it warm. Anywhere the limbs were damaged, the sap had frozen in place keeping the wound safe until it could heal. It was just as fascinating as the snow that sat on top.

Seek to find that which is underneath! You will not regret it, I PROMISE!

Ephesians 1:13-14
And you also were included in Christ when you heard the message of truth, the gospel of your salvation. When you believed, you were marked in him with a seal, the promised Holy Spirit, who is a deposit guaranteeing our inheritance until the redemption of those who are God's possession—to the praise of his glory.

Mary Remembers

I woke up really late this morning, a problem I will pay for tonight for sure lol. When I finally roused myself out of bed, I realized I needed an extra-large coffee just to function, so I got out my best extra-large cup and brewed a double batch to fill it. Grabbing my hat because it appears to be a bad hair day as well, I looked out the window to see the large snowflakes falling to the ground and for a moment my heart sank. I'm a winter lover, and I can honestly say I'm done for the season, I've had enough. It's time for the snow to stop falling and let Spring in! As quickly as that thought entered my brain, I was reminded of a day, 52 years and 7 days ago to be precise, when a young woman was driven by family to a hospital in Colorado to deliver her fifth child. There was already six inches on the ground and another ten were expected in the Spring blizzard of 1968. They made it to the hospital, and I was born in the elevator as it opened to the labor and delivery floor of the hospital. I soon realized that if I could survive that, this few inches of snow in the middle of April would not be able to keep me down and depressed. It was actually a day to be cherished.

As I continued my stroll down memory lane, no I don't remember my birth, but I do remember most of my birthdays lol, God spoke two simple words...

"Remember Luke."

As soon as I heard the words, I knew what God was pointing me to... Mary's story...

Because Luke had likely never met Jesus, the information found in his gospel came from his interviews of the people who lived it. Mary would have been in her late 70's or 80's when she was interviewed; by then she had lost her husband, watched one son be beaten and crucified, and another martyred for his belief in the first. More than likely she would have been in hiding when she sat down with Dr. Luke. By the time Mary travelled down memory lane with Luke, she had seen and done amazing things. She had tasted hardship the rest of us would likely run and hide from.

Because I had just recently watched Mel Gibson's "Passion of the Christ," I knew that there was a piece of Mary's story I needed to be focusing on, the fulfillment of Simeon's words, *"... And a sword will pierce your own soul too." Luke 2:35.* Simeon was prophesying that when Christ's side would be pierced, Mary would feel the same pain. Though it is not written in John 19:34, I have no doubt that when the soldier pierced the side of Jesus with his spear, Mary felt the intense pain of losing her first born child; a pain so severe, it likely pierced her side and doubled her over.

What strikes me the most is that when we read Mary's words, as penned by Luke, we see the joy of a woman called by God to do the impossible. We don't see the pain of a mother who has lost everything, instead we see a woman who celebrated every moment she was blessed to have been given. It's all about perspective.

 Yes, it's snowing in April, and freezing all of the flowers that were just starting to pop up, but if we were able to get out of bed today, we have been given an incredible gift that deserves to be celebrated as well as the one who gave it to us. No matter what difficulty you may be going through at this very moment, cherish the fact that you have a Savior willing to and capable of carrying the weight of whatever is trying to drag you down.

He loves us all that much!

Joel 2:28-29
And afterward, I will pour out my Spirit on all people. Your sons and daughters will prophesy, your old men will dream dreams, your young men will see visions. Even on my servants, both men and women, I will pour out my Spirit in those days.

Why Do We Choose Hurt?

Because Tyler has really thin white hair, and likely has some albino in him as well, he can't control his temperature the way most dogs do. We have had to be really careful keeping him out of extreme heat or cold situations. In the wintertime this wrestling match takes place in front of the fireplace. Even though he's panting, he won't leave it; he prefers to sleep right next to the flames. With the temperatures in the teens today, we started the fire for the first time since we brought Jake home, and now Tyler is trying to teach Jake the fine art of fireplace sleeping. Jake stayed for a little while, but as soon as he began panting, he got up and moved away; Tyler stayed right where he was.

I was scratching my head over what to do when God spoke…

"Why do you continue to do what hurts you?"

I usually don't realize I'm hurting myself until it's too late.

"But then you will go back and do it again. Why?"

At first, it's because I know I can do it better the next time, but then, it becomes a comfortable habit. Habits are hard to break.

"How I wish you would follow the plans I have for you. You could avoid so much pain."

As God spoke, I couldn't help but think of the story of Hosea and Gomer. God calls Hosea to marry a prostitute and he chooses Gomer. They have a few children and a seemingly good life when Hosea goes back to her old ways leaving Hosea to raise the children on his own. While it had to be incredibly difficult for Hosea, it was worse for Gomer. Her choices led her back to the familiar pain of prostitution, but then something happens (Scripture doesn't tell us) and Gomer is being auctioned off to the highest bidder; I can't imagine the hurt going on inside her. Out of the blue Hosea shows up and buys her back and takes her home.

We don't have to choose hurt anymore. We have been given the gift of Grace, we only have to accept it the way Gomer did. God's plan for our lives is better than anything we could ever come up with on our own. The world may be in turmoil and spinning out of control, but we don't have to be. We have been offered so much more. Yes it's hard, yes it's confusing at times, and yes we are going to make mistakes every now and then.

Don't lose faith and... CHOOSE HOPE!

Jeremiah 29:10-12
This is what the Lord says: "When seventy years are completed for Babylon, I will come to you and fulfill my good promise to bring you back to this place. For I know the plans I have for you," declares the Lord, "plans to prosper you and not to harm you, plans to give you hope and a future. Then you will call on me and come and pray to me, and I will listen to you.

The Ends Justify The Means?

Many of you know we live in the house my husband's grandfather built. Before we moved here, we would come visit grandpa as often as possible. In the wintertime he would always tell us to be careful starting our vehicles. Neighborhood as well as wild cats would sleep by the engine block to stay warm at night. Over his 70+ years in this home he had accidentally injured and even killed quite a few cats.

We moved in with dogs, so we didn't see very many cats at first. But they soon realized that our dogs were on ropes when they were outside, and therefore unable to give chase. I had to stop feeding the birds because the cats would wait until the birds were eating and then pounce on the easy meal. Now I have never been a fan of cats, I'm a dog person through and through, so I wasn't always diligent in checking the engine before I fired up a vehicle. I would chase the cats with a broom if they got too close to the house and caused the dogs to bark. If I was on my lawnmower, I would chase them off the property. While I never killed or injured any of them, I firmly believed that the ends would have justified the means. If you don't want to be chased with a lawnmower, don't be on the property on mowing day. Not in the mood to have a turkey nip at your tail, don't follow it into a bush (yes, I laughed hard when I saw that one). If a cat got hurt or killed it was their fault for being stupid.

God has been doing a work in me lately that has been really tough to walk through. So, when I saw the new neighborhood orange tabby while mowing today, I had to laugh, because I knew God was about to speak…

"Are you going to chase that cat with the mower?"

No.

"Why not, it's on your property? It's going to have your dogs barking up a storm in a few minutes."

The cat isn't hurting anything. It's just hunting voles and chipmunks.

"Is that the only reason?"

No. It's one of your creatures and you love it. Hurting it would be me intentionally hurting you.

"That's my girl!"

I've lived a very long time believing that as long as the ends justified the means, the mistreatment of people was okay. It was usually their fault anyway. I can't look at God's children that way anymore. He's teaching me to look at the world through His lens. It's daunting and it's gut wrenching, but it's also heartwarming and beautiful. God likely has you on a different journey, and you will disagree with me on this and that's okay; He has a unique journey for each of us to walk.

In this journey He has me on, I have had to scroll past some posts, and bite my tongue in certain conversations. I've cried heartbroken tears at the hatred and vitriol being tossed about from social media to the nightly news. But God, in His kindness, has softened my heart to the point that I am able to love without limits, I am able to look past the rage and the hurt to see God's beloved child. My prayer is that one day we can ALL look at each other with a lens created by God.

Much love my friends!

John 9:10-11
"How then were your eyes opened?" they asked. He replied, "The man they call Jesus made some mud and put it on my eyes. He told me to go to Siloam and wash. So I went and washed, and then I could see."

Loving Differences

God has taught me so much through the lens of these two dogs. Jake is the tan scrappy puppy, and Tyler is the white super chill old man. That's not the only differences they have, Jake is 95% trustworthy outside not on a leash while Tyler is not and has to be leashed. Tyler is 95% trustworthy inside when we are not home, but Jake is not and must be caged when we leave. Their personalities are so vastly different, it's been kind of fun to watch and learn. Jake has been bitten by a turtle hard enough to draw blood, and had a pretty severe shoulder injury, and yet he never whined or cried out in pain. Tyler on the other hand will get a scratch and cry like a baby until you recognize he's hurt. Tyler is a lap dog who likes his ears rubbed and Jake prefers the floor and belly rubs.

It's in these differences that God spoke...

"Do you love them differently or the same?"

I love them the same.

"Do their differences change the way you see them? Do you place one above the other?"

No, they are both an equal part of my family, I actually love the differences between them.

"That's how I feel about ALL of my children, even those who don't yet believe. I actually love the different things they bring to My table."

God created each of us to be a unique part of His kingdom and He love us all the same. It doesn't matter what our doctrine, political beliefs, skin color, job, or even belief in Him levels are, His love for us never changes. He hurts when we hurt, He laughs when we laugh, He loves even when we can't.

 Country singer Thomas Rhett has a song out right now called "Be a Light" and it is so apropos for where we are in society today, I think if God were to sing for us today, it would at least be the chorus of this one, "In a world full of hate, be a light. When you do somebody wrong, make it right. Don't hide in the dark, you were born to shine. In a world full of hate, be a light."

As this world continues to spin out of control, I am willfully choosing to love the differences in each of us. Will you?

John 13:34-35
"A new command I give you: Love one another. As I have loved you, so you must love one another. By this everyone will know that you are my disciples, if you love one another."

Where Is Your Heart?

There is such a joyous feeling when you can finally get back on your lawnmower... lolololol

Two years ago, Bob and I spent a week cleaning out these flower bed rock gardens. We replaced all of the soil, put weed and tree preventative measures in, and mulched it. Last year we planted some flowers and put some decorative barrels in there and had it looking beautiful. Through a series of LAME EXCUSES, we haven't done any work in them this year, and now they look like this. The weeds are all on the very top, but as you can see, they are a total eyesore! Every time I got near this area with the mower, all I could do was shake my head in shame.

And then God whispered... "This is what your heart looks like when you forget to surround yourself with My love for you. When you don't stop to feel My love, junk gets in and hides the beauty of what we share."

As Christians we can sometimes get so caught up in the busyness of being Christians that we forget the reason why we are. We ARE because HE loves us and nothing more. We go to church, we read our Bible, we volunteer, we do all that it takes RIGHT? Do we ever just sit back and just breathe in the love of God?

I hear a lot of people say that the Bible is an incredible rule book, it's the way to LIVE your life. Y'all it is SO much MORE than that!

Yes, there is phenomenal life application found in the Bible, but MORE than that, the Bible is a LOVE STORY and it deserves to be cherished as such. That Book describes in detail how God feels about us and what He is willing to go through to woo us to Him.

Riding on the mower today He gave me an opportunity to just be held and LOVED. I had a sense of peace when I got off the mower that I haven't felt in a while.

Next time we read the Bible, let's flip our perspective a little... instead of seeing how we need to act and what we need to do, let's stop and see all of the love God has for us and breathe that in instead. We need to feel the love of God so that we can reflect it to a dying world.

Song of Songs 4:9
You have stolen my heart, my sister, my bride; you have stolen my heart with one glance of your eyes, with one jewel of your necklace.

Thank You

Thank you so much for hanging out with me through these pages. I hope that at some point, you had a close encounter with the Creator and Lover of your soul. May He draw you to a deep, close and personal relationship with Him.

I hope that you have had as much enjoyment in reading these short glimpses into my world as I have had in writing them. If I could leave you with any encouragement, it would be that our Creator Redeemer God will walk with you through any and every emotion you have the capacity to feel. At your darkest moments, God will not only walk with you, but is willing to carry you through, allowing you to simply lean into His gentle embrace. When your joy knows no bounds, He will be there laughing and dancing right alongside you.

Until our journeys cross paths again, may you find enlightenment in the words and pages of God's Holy Writ and may those words give you the strength to be a light in this difficult and dark world.

Keep digging and studying my friends!

Lisa